This Book Belongs

to

....

....

from

....

....

SHIRLEY TEMPLE'S
Storybook

SHIRLEY

*Prepared under the Editorial
Supervision of* JOSETTE FRANK

TEMPLE'S
Storybook

RANDOM HOUSE, NEW YORK

TO MY CHILDREN AND YOURS

The publisher's thanks are extended to Longmans, Green and Company, Inc. for permission to use the version of ALI BABA AND THE FORTY THIEVES from Andrew Lang's *Arabian Nights*, Copyright, 1898, 1946, also to Noel Langley for permission to use an adaptation of his book, *The Land of Green Ginger*, and to David McKay Company, Inc. for the selection of illustrations by Arthur Rackham for *The Legend of Sleepy Hollow* by Washington Irving.

FOREWORD

As a child I loved reading fairy stories and tales of enchantment. Even today, in what has come to be called the Atomic Age, children enjoy hearing and reading about the magic world of fairy princes and princesses, of wicked witches who are punished for their bad deeds, of cleverness that is rewarded—in short, the same kinds of stories that their parents read when they were young. Certainly this is true of my own children.

Nor is there anything unusual, it seems to me, in a child's clinging to the idea of fairyland even as he is trying on a space helmet and dreaming of a trip to the moon, for to a child *everything* is new and a great experience. One such experience which in later years becomes a most cherished memory is the discovery of legendary tales handed down from generation to generation, of exploring the fascinating world of make-believe where wishes can come true. And who would deny any boy or girl this eternal right?

To children everywhere, therefore, I offer this book of favorite stories which I selected for my own television program, in the fond hope that they will find in it many hours of reading pleasure.

May 1958

Shirley Temple

CONTENTS

Beauty and the Beast

ILLUSTRATED BY PAUL BACON

ONCE UPON A TIME, in a very far-off country, there lived a merchant who had been so fortunate in all his undertakings that he was enormously rich. His ships sailed the seas bringing treasures from the far corners of the earth. He and his three daughters lived in great luxury in a fine house in the town.

But suddenly misfortune befell them. The merchant lost every ship he had upon the sea, either through pirates, shipwreck, or fire. Then he found that his clerks in distant countries, whom he trusted, had cheated him; and at last from great wealth he fell into the direst poverty.

All he had left was a little cottage in a desolate place in the forest, and to this he was forced to retreat with his daughters, who were in despair at the idea of leading such a different life. Now they found that they were left alone, and that their former friends who had been so numerous while they were rich, showed no intention of offering them any help.

As they were now too poor to have servants, the girls had to work hard. They complained constantly at having to live without the luxuries and amusements of their former life; only the youngest one tried to be brave and cheerful. She had been as sad as anyone when misfortune first overtook her father, but she soon set to work to make the best of things. She tried to amuse her father and to persuade her sisters to join her in dancing and singing. Because she was so cheerful, they declared that this miserable life was all she was fit for. She was really far prettier and cleverer than they; indeed, she was so lovely to look at that she was always called Beauty.

After two years, when they were all beginning to get used to their new life, the merchant received news that one of his ships, which he had believed lost, had come safely into port with a rich cargo. The daughters, thinking that now they would be rich again, wanted to set out directly for the town. But their father, who was more prudent, begged them to wait a little; he would go by himself to make inquiries.

So they loaded their father with requests that he bring them jewels and dresses which it would have taken a fortune to buy. Only Beauty did not ask for anything. Her father said: "And what shall I bring for you, Beauty?"

"The only thing I wish is for you to come home safely," she answered.

But her father thought there must be some pretty thing she would want, so he begged her to name it.

"Well, dear father," she said, "as you insist upon it, I beg that you will bring me a rose. I have not seen one since we came here, and I love them so much."

The merchant set out and reached the town as quickly as possible, only to find that his ship had been seized and sold to pay his debts. So after months of trouble and expense he started back to the cottage poorer than ever. To make matters worse, it was mid-winter now and he was obliged to leave the town in the most terrible weather, so that by the time he was within a few leagues of his home he was almost exhausted with cold and fatigue. He was in the deep forest when night overtook him. The falling snow had covered up every trail, and he did not know which way to turn.

At length he made out some sort of path, and this led him into a lovely garden, at the end of which stood a splendid castle, its windows blazing with light. It seemed to the merchant very strange that no snow had fallen in the garden, which was in full bloom. He walked on in wonderment until he came to the great door of the castle. A golden horn hung on a chair beside it. After a moment's hesitation the merchant put the horn to his lips and blew it. At once the door opened, and he stepped into a wide and noble hall brilliantly lighted with golden lamps. He called aloud but there was no answer. There seemed to be nobody in all this vast and splendid palace. Going further into the great room he found a fire blazing on the hearth. A couch was drawn up cozily and before it a table had been set for one. Thinking that this must be prepared for someone who was expected, the merchant sat down to wait.

But he was terribly hungry and wished there were someone whom he could ask to give him something to eat. He glanced again at the litle table and saw that a delicious dinner had been placed on it. Now an unseen hand lifted the covers from the dishes, and the chair was moved back a little to receive him. "It seems," he thought, "this dinner is meant for me." As he had eaten nothing for twenty-four hours, he lost no time in beginning his meal, hoping that he might soon have an opportunity of thanking his considerate host, whoever it might be. But no one appeared. Now he noticed that the couch was made up into a bed. Taking off his boots and jacket, the merchant fell into the bed and was soon fast asleep. When he awoke completely refreshed, he saw that a complete outfit of handsome new clothes had replaced his worn ones. There was still no sign of anybody, even though a fresh meal of dainty cakes and fruit had been

12

placed upon the little table at his elbow. After satisfying his appetite, he dressed and went down into the garden. And here, though it was winter everywhere else, the sun shone, the birds sang, flowers bloomed, and the air was soft and sweet. Along the path a hedge of beautiful roses reminded him of his promise to Beauty. He stopped and had just plucked one to take to her when he was startled by a strange noise

behind him. Turning around, he was faced by a frightful Beast, which seemed very angry and said in a terrible voice:

"Who told you that you might gather my roses? Was it not enough that I sheltered you in my palace and was kind to you? Is this the way you thank me, by robbing me of my roses? But your insolence shall not go unpunished."

The merchant, terrified by these furious words, dropped the rose and, throwing himself on his knees, cried: "Pardon me, noble sir. I am truly grateful to you for your hospitality, which was so magnificent that I could not imagine you would be offended by my taking such a little thing as a rose."

But the Beast was still angry. "You are very ready with excuses and flattery," he cried; "but that will not save you from the death you deserve."

"Alas!" thought the merchant. "If my daughter Beauty could only know what danger her rose has brought me into!"

And in despair he told the Beast of his misfortunes, and the reason of his journey, and especially of Beauty's request.

"A king's ransom would hardly have procured all that my other daughters asked," he said; "but I thought that I might at least take Beauty her rose. I beg you to forgive me, for you see I meant no harm."

The Beast thought for a moment, and then he said:

"I will spare you on one condition—that is, that you will give me one of your daughters."

"Ah!" cried the merchant. "Even if I were cruel enough to buy my own life at the cost of one of my children's what excuse could I invent to bring her here?"

"No excuse!" thundered the Beast. "She must come of her own free will if she loves you enough to want to save your life. On no other condition will I have her. Return in a month with one of your daughters if one of them is courageous enough to come back with you and stay here, in order to let you go free. Otherwise you must return alone. And do not imagine that you can hide from me," added the Beast grimly, "for if you do not return in a month I will come and fetch you!"

The merchant accepted this proposal, though he did not really intend to bring any of his daughters. He wanted only to go and see them for the last time.

"Now farewell," said the Beast. "Take a rose to Beauty and remember your promise!"

The merchant was only too glad when the Beast left him. He gathered up Beauty's rose, and went off swiftly to the cottage in the forest.

His daughters rushed to meet him, eager to know the result of

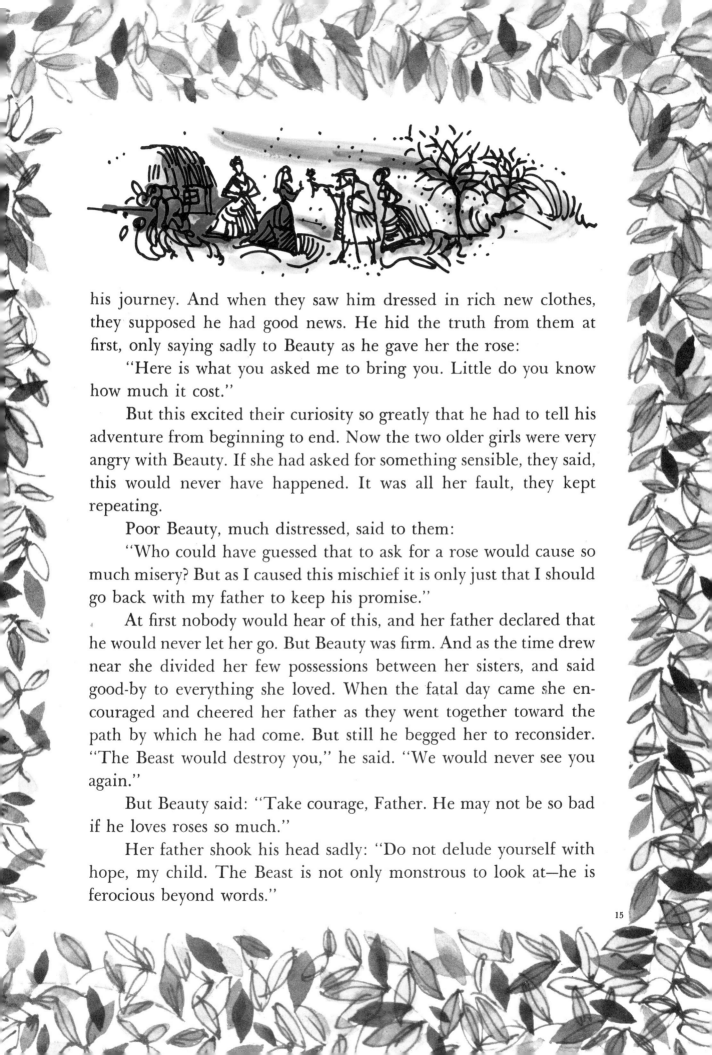

his journey. And when they saw him dressed in rich new clothes, they supposed he had good news. He hid the truth from them at first, only saying sadly to Beauty as he gave her the rose:

"Here is what you asked me to bring you. Little do you know how much it cost."

But this excited their curiosity so greatly that he had to tell his adventure from beginning to end. Now the two older girls were very angry with Beauty. If she had asked for something sensible, they said, this would never have happened. It was all her fault, they kept repeating.

Poor Beauty, much distressed, said to them:

"Who could have guessed that to ask for a rose would cause so much misery? But as I caused this mischief it is only just that I should go back with my father to keep his promise."

At first nobody would hear of this, and her father declared that he would never let her go. But Beauty was firm. And as the time drew near she divided her few possessions between her sisters, and said good-by to everything she loved. When the fatal day came she encouraged and cheered her father as they went together toward the path by which he had come. But still he begged her to reconsider. "The Beast would destroy you," he said. "We would never see you again."

But Beauty said: "Take courage, Father. He may not be so bad if he loves roses so much."

Her father shook his head sadly: "Do not delude yourself with hope, my child. The Beast is not only monstrous to look at—he is ferocious beyond words."

To this, Beauty replied: "Is it not possible, Father, for a beast to be tamed?"

When they had nearly reached the palace they saw that it was brilliantly lit from the roof to the ground. The garden was hung with lanterns, and soft music sounded from the courtyard.

"The Beast must be very hungry," said Beauty, trying to laugh, "if he makes all this rejoicing over the arrival of his prey."

But, in spite of her fears, she could not help admiring all the wonderful scene before her.

Again, as before, the great door of the palace opened by itself and closed after them. The merchant led Beauty into the room he had been in before. There they found a blazing fire, and the table daintily spread with a magnificent feast for two.

The merchant knew that this was meant for them. Beauty was too frightened to be hungry, but feared it would anger the Beast if they ignored his hospitality. They had barely finished their meal when the noise of the Beast's footsteps was heard approaching. Beauty clung to her father in terror. But when the Beast really appeared she made a great effort to hide her horror, and saluted him respectfully.

This evidently pleased the Beast. He looked at her in silence. Then he said:

"Good evening, old man. Good evening, Beauty."

The merchant was too terrified to reply, but Beauty answered sweetly:

"Good evening, sir."

"I am the Beast," he said. "You will call me that, please."

"Good evening, Beast," Beauty said, politely.

"Have you come willingly?" asked the Beast. "Will you be content to stay here when your father goes away?"

Beauty answered bravely that she was quite prepared to stay.

"I am pleased with you," said the Beast. "And as you have come of your own accord, you may stay. You will find everything in readiness for your comfort. If you find anything lacking you have only to speak your wish and it will be fulfilled." Then, turning to the merchant, he said: "Upon your return home you will find a sack filled with gold awaiting you. You may consider it a remembrance from Beauty to her sisters."

Then in a stern voice: "Now leave this palace, merchant. And do not expect ever to return to it." Then he went away, after saying, "Good-by, Beauty; good-by, old man."

Now the merchant clung to Beauty, weeping: "Oh, my child, I cannot leave you alone here. I fear I shall never see you again."

But Beauty comforted him: "We must not lose hope, Father. Go now. Go quickly, or my heart will break." Slowly her father moved toward the great door. It opened and then closed after him. Now Beauty was alone. She sank down on the couch and wept quietly.

Suddenly the silence in the room was broken by the sound of soft music. Beauty arose and walked toward the room from which the music seemed to be coming. At the door she paused. On it, in beautiful letters, were the words: "Beauty's Room." Greatly surprised, she entered and looked about in wonder. The room was filled with beautiful things; on the table lay heaps of dazzling jewels and in the closets were dresses fit for a queen. Everywhere were things for her comfort. Beauty went from treasure to treasure, looking at them in bewilderment. Finally her eyes rested on a small picture in

a golden frame, hanging on the wall. It was a picture of a young prince, and Beauty thought she had never seen anyone so handsome.

Now she began to feel very sleepy, and lay down on the snowy bed that was prepared for her. She fell asleep at once. And as she slept, she had a dream. She dreamed that she was walking by a brook bordered with trees, when the handsome young prince of the picture came to her and said, "Ah, Beauty! You are not so unfortunate as you suppose. Here you will be rewarded for all you have suffered elsewhere. Your every wish shall be granted. Only try to find me out, no matter how I may be disguised. I am a prisoner here in the castle of the Beast. Find me, and set me free."

"Tell me how to find you, dear Prince," said Beauty.

"Find me with your heart," he answered, "and do not trust too much to your eyes. Above all, do not desert me until you have saved me from my cruel misery. Without you I shall die."

When Beauty awoke she found her dressing table set out with everything she could possibly want. When she had bathed and dressed she found a delicious breakfast awaiting her. She thought of her dream prince, and looked again at the picture to see if he was the same.

"He said that I should find him," said Beauty to herself. "It seems, then, that this horrible Beast keeps him a prisoner. How can I set him free? I wonder why he told me not to trust too much to my eyes? I don't understand it. But, then, it was only a dream."

To pass the time she began to explore some of the many rooms of the palace, half hoping to find the prince of her dream. The first she entered was lined with mirrors, and Beauty saw herself reflected on every side. Then a bracelet which was hanging from a chandelier caught her eye, and on taking it down she was greatly surprised to find that it held a portrait of her unknown prince, just as she had seen him in her dream. With great delight she slipped the bracelet on her arm. Then she passed through into a room which contained every musical instrument. The next room was a library, and it seemed to her that a whole lifetime would not be enough even to read the names of the books, there were so many. So the day passed and it was growing dusk; wax candles in diamond and ruby candlesticks were beginning to light themselves in every room. And still Beauty had not seen anyone nor heard a single voice.

She found her supper served just at the time she wished to have it. But she began to be rather lonely, and to wonder when she would see the Beast again.

Presently she heard him coming, and she could not help trembling. Perhaps he would be angry with her.

However, he did not seem at all ferocious, and only said gruffly: "Good evening, Beauty."

She answered cheerfully and managed to conceal her terror. Then the Beast asked if she had found everything to her liking, and whether she thought she could be happy in his palace. Beauty answered that everything was so beautiful and he was so kind that she would be very hard to please if she could not be happy here. Beauty began to think that the Beast was not nearly so terrible as she had

supposed at first. As he got up to leave her, he said in his gruff voice:

"I know I am only a Beast. Tell me, honestly, do you not think me very ugly?"

"Yes, Beast—since you wish the truth," said Beauty.

"Does my appearance horrify you?" he asked more gently.

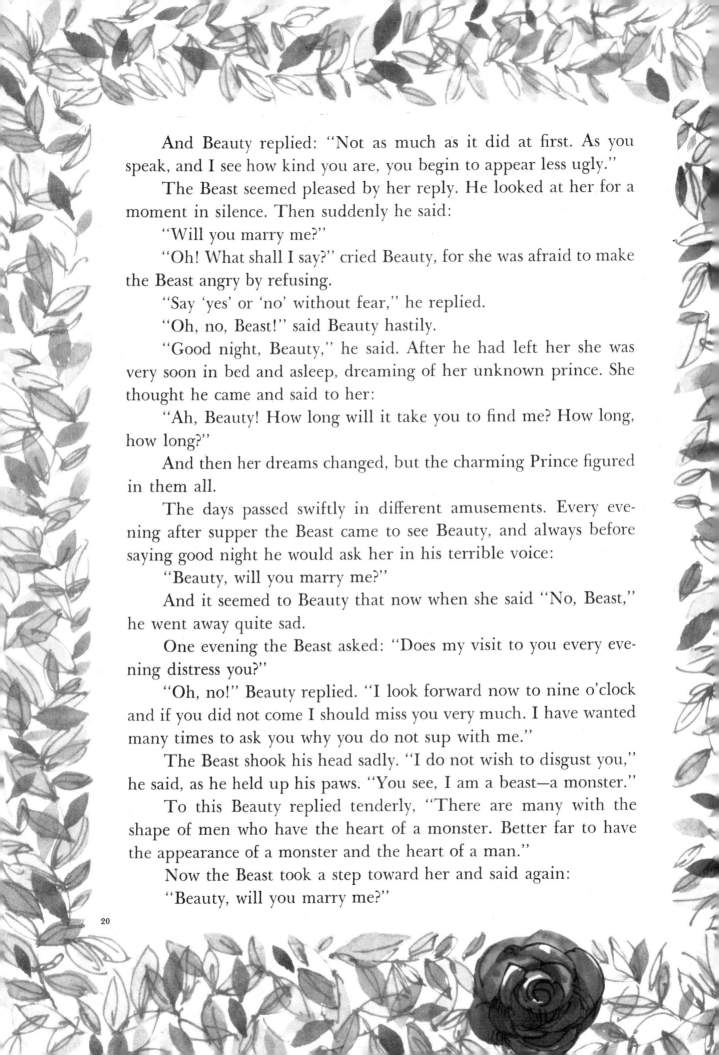

And Beauty replied: "Not as much as it did at first. As you speak, and I see how kind you are, you begin to appear less ugly."

The Beast seemed pleased by her reply. He looked at her for a moment in silence. Then suddenly he said:

"Will you marry me?"

"Oh! What shall I say?" cried Beauty, for she was afraid to make the Beast angry by refusing.

"Say 'yes' or 'no' without fear," he replied.

"Oh, no, Beast!" said Beauty hastily.

"Good night, Beauty," he said. After he had left her she was very soon in bed and asleep, dreaming of her unknown prince. She thought he came and said to her:

"Ah, Beauty! How long will it take you to find me? How long, how long?"

And then her dreams changed, but the charming Prince figured in them all.

The days passed swiftly in different amusements. Every evening after supper the Beast came to see Beauty, and always before saying good night he would ask her in his terrible voice:

"Beauty, will you marry me?"

And it seemed to Beauty that now when she said "No, Beast," he went away quite sad.

One evening the Beast asked: "Does my visit to you every evening distress you?"

"Oh, no!" Beauty replied. "I look forward now to nine o'clock and if you did not come I should miss you very much. I have wanted many times to ask you why you do not sup with me."

The Beast shook his head sadly. "I do not wish to disgust you," he said, as he held up his paws. "You see, I am a beast—a monster."

To this Beauty replied tenderly, "There are many with the shape of men who have the heart of a monster. Better far to have the appearance of a monster and the heart of a man."

Now the Beast took a step toward her and said again:

"Beauty, will you marry me?"

Beauty was silent, for she hated to hurt him. At last she said gently, "No, Beast," and he left her in great distress.

So matters went on for many months, until at last, happy as she was, Beauty began to long for the sight of her father and sisters. One night, seeing her look very sad, the Beast asked her what troubled her. Beauty was no longer afraid of him, for she knew that he was really gentle in spite of his ferocious looks and his dreadful voice. So she answered that she was longing to see her home once more. Upon hearing this the Beast seemed sadly distressed, and cried miserably:

"Ah! Beauty, have you the heart to desert an unhappy Beast? What more do you want to make you happy? Is it because you hate me that you want to escape?"

"No, dear Beast," answered Beauty softly. "I do not hate you, and I should be very sorry never to see you any more. But I long to see my father again. Let me go for a week, and I promise to come back to you and stay for the rest of my life."

The Beast pleaded:

"I need you, Beauty. Without you I shall die."

Slowly Beauty repeated his words. "I have heard those words before," she said.

"They are true," said the Beast. "But I cannot refuse you anything you ask, even though it should cost me my life. Take the four boxes you will find in the room next to your own, and fill them with everything you wish to take with you. But remember your promise and come back when the week is over, for if you do not you will find your faithful Beast dead. You will not need any chariot to bring you back. Only say good-by to your father and sisters the night before you come away, and when you have gone to bed turn this ring around upon your finger and say firmly: 'I wish to go back to my palace and see my Beast again.'"

Then, taking a rose from a vase on the table, he said:

"Take this rose with you. It will remain fresh and alive for a week. Then it will begin to wilt. Its petals will fall and it will be dying. You will know then, if you do not return, that I too am dying.'' She saw that he was weeping.

"Good night, Beauty. Fear nothing, sleep peacefully, and before long you shall see your father once more.''

As soon as Beauty was alone she hastened to fill the boxes with all the rare and precious things she saw about her. Then she went to bed, and dreamed again of her beloved Prince.

A strange sound woke her—someone was speaking not very far away. Opening her eyes, she found herself in a room she had never seen before. Where could she be? She got up and dressed hastily, wondering by what magic the Beast had transported her to this strange place. Suddenly she heard her father's voice, and rushed out and greeted him joyfully. Her sisters were all astonished at her appearance, and there was no end to the questions they asked her. She had also much to hear about what had happened to them while she was away. But when they heard that she had come to be with them

only for a short time, and then must go back to the Beast's palace forever, they lamented loudly.

Then Beauty asked her father what he thought could be the

meaning of her strange dreams, and why the Prince constantly begged her not to trust to appearances. After much consideration he answered: "You tell me yourself that the Beast, frightful as he is, loves you dearly and deserves your love and gratitude for his gentleness and kindness. I think the Prince must mean that you ought to reward the Beast by doing as he wishes, in spite of his ugliness."

The time passed quickly, but Beauty often thought of the palace, of her dream Prince and of the kind and thoughtful Beast. She would not be sorry when the week was over and she would return to them. Her sisters seemed to have got quite used to being without her, and even found her rather in the way. But they had, nevertheless, been scheming together to keep her from going back, for they hoped that her failure to return would cause the Beast to die, and they might then take possession of his palace and his riches. "Why should *she* have more than we have?" they asked each other. So they persuaded their father to beg Beauty to stay a few days longer. Beauty found it hard to refuse him, for he seemed so unhappy at the thought of her leaving. "A few more days will do no harm," she told herself.

Then one night she had a dismal dream. She thought she heard groans which seemed to come from some bushes hiding the entrance of a cave, and running quickly to see what could be the matter, she found the Beast stretched out upon his side. He reproached her faintly with being the cause of his distress, and to her horror she saw that he was dying.

Beauty was terrified by this dream. When she awoke the next morning she suddenly saw that the rose at her bedside was wilting. Already some of the petals had fallen to the table. Hastily she got out of bed and reached for her ring on the table. It was not there. Her sisters had taken it while she slept, and were even now trying out its powers to see if it would work for their wishes. When they found that the ring only played tricks on them they fell to quarreling. Hearing this, Beauty hurried in to them. She picked up the precious ring which they had hastily thrown to the floor. Quickly she slipped the ring on her finger, turned it around as she had been told to do, and said:

"I wish to go back to the palace, and see my Beast again."

Instantly she was in the palace once more. Everything was just as before. But Beauty thought she had never known such a long day, for she was so anxious to see the Beast again that she felt as if supper-time would never come.

But when nine o'clock came and and no Beast appeared she was really frightened. So, after listening and waiting for a long time she ran down into the garden where she searched for him everywhere in vain. At last, quite tired, she saw that she was standing opposite the shady path she had seen in her dream. She rushed down it, and sure enough, there was the cave, and in it lay the Beast—asleep, as Beauty thought. She ran up and called to him, but to her horror he did not move or open his eyes.

"Oh! he is dead; and it is all my fault," said Beauty, crying bitterly. She threw herself down beside him and, taking one of his paws in her hand, stroked his head. He opened his eyes slowly.

"Oh! Beast, how you frightened me!" she cried. "I never knew how much I loved you until just now, when I feared I was too late to save your life."

"Can you really love such an ugly creature as I am?" said the Beast faintly. "Ah! Beauty, you came only just in time. I was dying because I thought you had forgotten your promise."

"No, dear Beast," said Beauty. "You shall not die. And I do not wish to live without you. I love you . . . and I want to marry you!"

As she spoke a blaze of light sprang up before the windows of the palace; fireworks crackled and guns banged, and across the avenue of orange trees, in letters all made of fireflies, was written: "Long live the Prince and his Bride!"

Turning to ask the Beast what it could all mean, Beauty found that he had disappeared; in his place stood the handsome Prince of the picture and her dream.

But Beauty cried, "Where is my Beast?"

"He is gone forever," said the Prince.

"No, no," said Beauty. "I want my Beast. I must go to find him."

"Wait, Beauty!" the Prince said. "Look at me. *I* was the Beast. A magician cast a spell over me and condemned me to remain in that form until a beautiful young woman should, of her own free will, consent to marry me. You, dear Beauty, have broken the spell."

"But why were you so punished?" Beauty asked.

"Because I was proud and thoughtless, vain and selfish, he made me look as I really was. But during the long years of my agony, I learned to know what it is to live unloved. And the pride and selfishness burned away until you were able to love me—even as the Beast."

"With all my heart," Beauty said. And they turned and went together into the beautifully lighted palace.

Their marriage was celebrated the very next day with the utmost splendor, and Beauty and the Prince lived happily ever after.

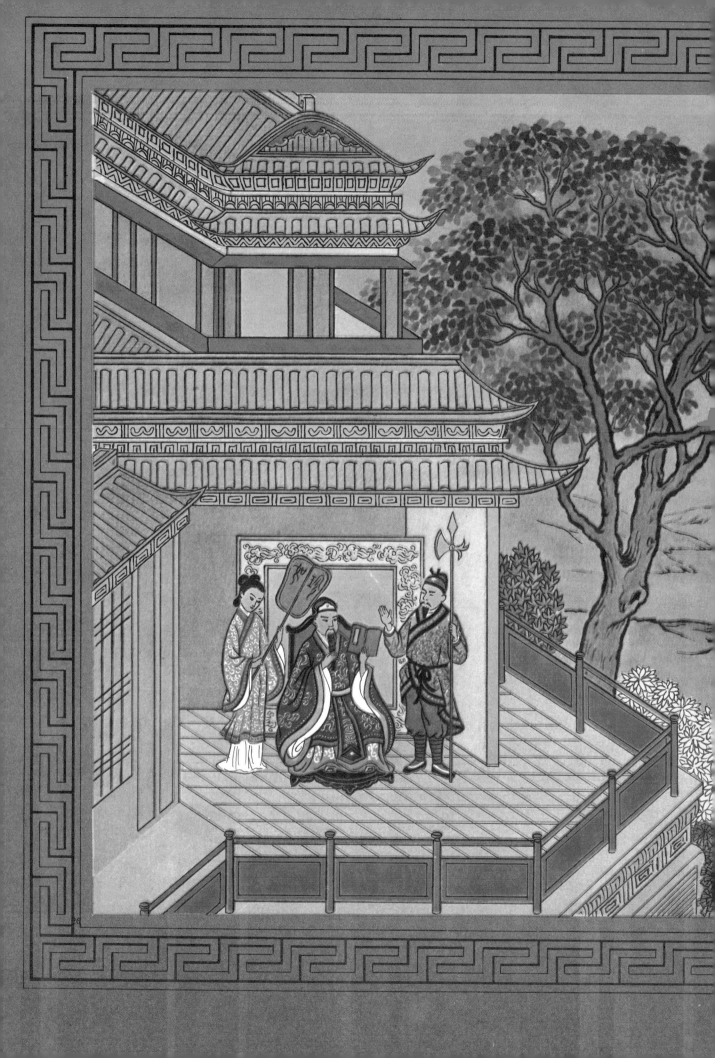

The Nightingale

ILLUSTRATED BY JEANYEE WONG

IN CHINA, YOU MUST KNOW, the Emperor is Chinese, and all whom he has about him are Chinese too. The story I am about to tell happened a good many years ago, but that's just why it's worth-while to hear it before it is forgotten. The Emperor's palace was the most splendid in the world; it was made entirely of porcelain, very costly, but so delicate and brittle that one had to take care how one touched it. In the garden were to be seen the most wonderful flowers, and to the costliest of them silver bells were tied, which sounded, so that nobody should pass by without noticing the flowers. Yes, everything in the Emperor's garden was admirably arranged. And it extended so far that the gardener himself did not know where the end was. If a man went on and on, he came into a glorious forest with high trees and deep lakes. The wood extended straight down to the sea, which was blue and deep; great ships could sail to beneath the branches of the trees; and in the trees lived a Nightingale, which sang so splendidly that even a poor fisherman, who had many other things to do, stopped still and listened, when he had gone out at night to throw out his nets, and heard the Nightingale.

"How beautiful that is!" he said; but he was obliged to attend to his work, and thus forgot the bird. But when in the next night the bird sang again, and the fisherman heard it, he exclaimed again, "How beautiful that is!"

From all the countries of the world travelers came to the city of the Emperor, and admired it, and the palace, and the garden, but when they heard the Nightingale, they said, "That is the best of all!"

And the travelers told of it when they came home; and the learned men wrote many books about the town, the palace, and the garden.

But they did not forget the Nightingale; that was placed highest of all; and those who were poets wrote most magnificent poems about the Nightingale in the wood by the deep lake.

The books went through all the world, and a few of them once came to the Emperor. He sat in his golden chair, and read, and read. Every moment he nodded his head, for it pleased him to peruse the masterly descriptions of the city, the palace, and the garden. "But the Nightingale is the best of all," it stood written there.

"What's that?" exclaimed the Emperor. "I don't know the Nightingale at all! Is there such a bird in my empire, and even in my garden? I've never heard of that. To think that I should have to learn such a thing for the first time from books!"

And hereupon he called his cavalier.

"There is said to be a wonderful bird here called a Nightingale," said the Emperor. "They say it is the best thing in all my great empire. Why have I never heard anything about it?"

"I have never heard him named," replied the cavalier. "He has never been introduced at Court."

"I command that he shall appear this evening, and sing before me," said the Emperor.

"I have never heard him mentioned," said the cavalier. "I will seek for him. I will find him."

But where was he to be found? The cavalier ran up and down all the staircases, through halls and passages, but no one among all those whom he met had heard talk of the Nightingale.

Then there was a great inquiry after the wonderful Nightingale, which all the world knew excepting the people at Court.

At last they met with a poor little girl in the kitchen, who said:

"The Nightingale? I know it well; yes, it can sing gloriously. Every evening I get leave to carry my poor sick mother the scraps from the table. She lives down by the strand, and when I get back and am tired, and rest in the wood, then I hear the Nightingale sing. And then the water comes into my eyes, and it is just as if my mother kissed me."

"Little kitchen-girl," said the cavalier, "I will get you a place in the kitchen, with permission to see the Emperor dine, if you will lead us to the Nightingale."

So they all went out into the wood where the Nightingale was accustomed to sing. When they were in the midst of their journey a cow began to low.

"Oh!" cried the Court pages. "Now we have it! That shows a wonderful power in so small a creature! I have certainly heard it before."

"No, those are cows lowing," said the little kitchen-girl. "We are a long way from the place yet."

Now the frogs began to croak in the marsh.

"Glorious!" said the music master. "Now I hear it—it sounds just like little church bells."

"No, those are frogs," said the little kitchen-maid. "But now I think we shall soon hear it."

And then the Nightingale began to sing.

"That is it!" exclaimed the little girl. "Listen, listen! And yonder it sits."

And she pointed to a little gray bird up in the boughs.

"Is it possible?" cried the cavalier. "I should never have thought it looked like that. How simple it looks! It must certainly have lost its color at seeing such grand people around."

"Little Nightingale!" called the little kitchen-maid, quite loudly. "Our gracious Emperor wishes you to sing before him."

"With the greatest pleasure," replied the Nightingale, and began to sing most delightfully.

"It sounds just like glass bells," said the cavalier. "And see how its little throat is working! It's strange that we should never have heard it before. That bird will be a great success at Court."

"Shall I sing once more before the Emperor?" asked the Nightingale, for it thought the Emperor was present.

"My excellent little Nightingale," said the cavalier, "I have great pleasure in inviting you to a Court festival this evening, when you shall charm his Imperial Majesty with your beautiful singing."

"My song sounds best in the green woods," replied the Nightingale. Still it came willingly when it heard what the Emperor wished.

In the midst of the great hall, where the Emperor sat, a golden perch had been placed on which the Nightingale was to sit. The whole Court was there, and the little cook-maid had got leave to stand behind the door, as she had now received the title of a real Court cook. All were in full dress, and all looked at the little gray bird, to which the Emperor nodded.

And the Nightingale sang so gloriously that the tears came into the Emperor's eyes, and the tears ran down over his cheeks; and when the Nightingale sang still more sweetly, it went straight to the heart. The Emperor was so pleased that he said the Nightingale should have his golden slipper to wear around its neck. But the Nightingale declined this with thanks, saying it had already received a sufficient reward.

"I have seen tears in the Emperor's eyes—that is the real treasure

—to me. An Emperor's tears have a peculiar power. I am rewarded enough." And then it sang again with a sweet glorious voice.

"How wonderfully talented it is!" exclaimed the ladies who stood round about, and they gargled their throats with water whenever anyone spoke to them. They thought they could be nightingales too. The lackeys and chambermaids reported that they were satisfied too; and that was saying a good deal, for they are the most difficult to please. In short, the Nightingale achieved a real success.

It was now to remain at Court, to have its own cage, with liberty to go out twice every day and once at night. Twelve servants were appointed to accompany it when the Nightingale went out. Each had a silken string which was fastened to the bird's leg and held very tight. There was really no pleasure in an excursion of that kind.

One day the Emperor received a large parcel on which was written, "The Nightingale."

"There we have a new book about this celebrated bird," said the Emperor.

But it was not a book. It was a little work of art contained in a box, an artificial nightingale which sang like a natural one and was brilliantly ornamented with diamonds, rubies, and sapphires. As soon as the artificial bird was wound up, he could sing, and then his tail moved up and down and shone with silver and gold. Round his neck hung a little ribbon, and on that was written, "The Emperor of China's nightingale is poor compared to that of the Emperor of Japan."

"That is capital!" said everybody at Court, and the person who had brought the artificial bird immediately received the title, Imperial Head-Nightingale-Bringer.

"Now they must sing together; what a duet that will be!"

And so they had to sing together; but it did not sound very well, for the real Nightingale sang in its own way, and the artificial bird sang waltzes.

Now the artificial bird was to sing alone. It had just as much success as the real one, and was much handsomer to look at—it shone

THE EMPEROR OF CHINA'S NIGHTINGALE IS POOR COMPARED EMPEROR OF JAPAN

like bracelets and breastpins.

Three and thirty times over it sang the same piece, and yet it never tired. The people would gladly have heard it again, but the Emperor said that the living Nightingale ought to sing something now. But where was it? No one had noticed that it had flown away out of the open window, back to the green wood.

"What has become of it?" said the Emperor.

And all the courtiers abused the Nightingale, and declared that it was a very ungrateful creature.

"We have the best bird, after all," said they.

And so the artificial bird had to sing again, and that was the thirty-fourth time the courtiers listened to the same piece. For all that, they did not know it quite by heart, for it was a very difficult piece. The music master praised the bird particularly. Yes, he declared, it was better than a nightingale, not only because of its plumage and the many beautiful diamonds, but because of its inside workings as well.

"For you see, ladies and gentlemen," he said, "and above all, your Imperial Majesty, with a real nightingale one can never calculate what is coming, but in this artificial bird everything is settled. One can explain it; one can open it and make people understand where the waltzes come from, how they go, and how one follows up another."

"Exactly," they all agreed.

And the music master received permission to show the bird to the people on the following Sunday. The people were much pleased.

But the poor fisherman, who had heard the real Nightingale, said:

"It sounds pretty enough, and the melodies resemble each other, but there's something missing, though I don't know what."

The real Nightingale was banished from the country and empire. The artificial bird had its place on a silken cushion close to the Emperor's bed. All the presents it had received, gold and precious stones, were ranged about it. In title it had advanced to be the High Imperial After-Dinner-Singer, and in rank to number one on the left hand; for the Emperor considered the side on which the heart is placed to be the more important, and even in an Emperor the heart is on the left side.

So a whole year went by. The Emperor, the Court, and all the other Chinese knew every little twitter in the artificial bird's song by heart. But just for that reason it pleased them—they could sing it by themselves now, and they did so. The street boys sang, "Tsi-tsi-tsi-glug-glug!" and the Emperor himself sang it too. Yes, it was certainly famous.

But one evening, when the artificial bird was singing its best, and the Emperor lay in bed listening to it, something inside the bird said, "Whizz!" Something cracked. "Whir-r-r!" All the wheels ran round, and then the music stopped.

The Emperor immediately sprang out of bed, and sent for his physician; but what could *he* do? Then a watchmaker was sent for, and after a good deal of talking and investigation, the bird was repaired to some extent; but the watchmaker said that the bird must be carefully treated, for its springs were badly worn, and it would be impossible to put in new ones without damage to the music. There was much sorrow when the people heard of this. Only once a year could the bird be permitted to sing, and even that was almost too much. But then the music master made a little speech, full of long words, in which he said the bird was just as good as before. And so, of course, everybody had to take his word for it.

Five years passed, and then a real calamity befell the whole nation. The Chinese were really fond of their Emperor, and now he was ill, and could not, it was said, live much longer. Already a new Emperor had been chosen, and the people stood about in the street and asked the cavalier how their old Emperor was doing. He shook his head.

Cold and pale lay the Emperor in his great gorgeous bed; the whole Court thought him dead, and each one ran to pay homage to the new ruler. The chamberlains ran out to talk it over, and the ladies' maids had a great coffee party. All about, in the halls and passages, cloth had been laid down so that no footsteps could be heard, and therefore it was quiet there, quite quiet. But the Emperor was not dead yet. He lay stiff and pale on the gorgeous bed with the long velvet curtains and the heavy gold tassels; high up, a window stood open, and the moon shone in upon the Emperor and the artificial bird.

The poor Emperor could hardly breathe; it was just as if something lay upon his chest, and had put on his golden crown, and held in one hand the Emperor's sword, and in the other his beautiful banner. And all around, from among the folds of the splendid velvet curtains, strange heads peered forth; a few very ugly, the rest quite lovely and mild. These were all the Emperor's bad and good deeds, that stood before him now that Death sat upon his heart.

"Do you remember this?" whispered one to the other. "Do you remember that?" and then they told him so much that the perspiration ran from his forehead.

"I did not know that!" said the Emperor. "Music! Music! The great Chinese drum," he cried, "so that I need not hear all they say!"

And they continued speaking, and Death nodded to all they said.

"Music! Music!" cried the Emperor. "You little precious golden bird, sing, sing! I have given you gold and costly presents; I have even hung my golden slipper around your neck—sing now, sing!"

But the bird stood still; no one was there to wind him up, and he could not sing without that. But Death continued to stare at the Emperor, and it was quiet, fearfully quiet.

Then suddenly there sounded from the window the most lovely song. It came from the little live Nightingale, that sat outside on the branch of a tree. It had heard of the Emperor's sad plight and had come to sing to him of comfort and hope. And as it sang the spectres grew paler and paler; the blood ran more quickly through the Emperor's weak limbs. Even Death listened, and said:

"Go on, little Nightingale, go on!"

And the Nightingale sang on and on. It sang of the quiet churchyard where the white roses grow, where the elder blossom smells sweet, and where the fresh grass is moistened by the tears of survivors. Then Death felt a longing to see his garden, and floated out of the window in the form of a cold white mist.

"Thanks! Thanks!" said the Emperor. "You heavenly little bird!

I know you well. I banished you from my country and empire, and yet you have charmed away the evil faces from my couch, and banished Death from my heart! How can I reward you?"

"You have rewarded me," replied the Nightingale. "I drew tears from your eyes when I sang the first time—I shall never forget that. Those are the jewels that rejoice a singer's heart. But now sleep and grow fresh and strong again. I will sing you something."

And it sang, and the Emperor fell into a sweet slumber. Ah! How mild and refreshing that sleep was! The sun shone upon him through the window when he awoke refreshed and restored. Not one of his servants had yet returned, for they all thought he was dead; only the Nightingale still sat beside him and sang.

"You must always stay with me," said the Emperor. "You shall sing as you please; and I'll break the artificial bird into a thousand pieces."

"Please do not do so," replied the Nightingale. "It did as well as it could; so keep it as you have done till now. As for me, I cannot build my nest in the palace. But let me come on the evenings when I feel inclined to do so. Then I will sit on the branch yonder by the window, and sing to you. I will sing of those who are happy and of those who suffer. I will sing of the good and evil that remains hidden around you. As a singing bird I must fly far around—to the poor fisherman, to the peasant's roof, to everyone who dwells far away from you and your court. I love your heart more than your crown, and I will come and sing to you—but one thing you must promise me."

"Everything!" said the Emperor; and he stood there in his imperial robes, which he had put on himself, and pressed his heavy gold sword to his heart.

"No, only one thing I beg of you: tell no one that you have a little bird who tells you everything. Then it will go all the better."

And the Nightingale flew away.

The servants came in to look to their dead Emperor, and—yes, there he stood, and the Emperor said, "Good morning!"

The Little Lame Prince

ILLUSTRATED BY DICK DODGE

YES, HE WAS THE MOST beautiful Prince that ever was born! Of course, since he was a Prince, people would say this, but it was really true. His bright eyes had an earnest expression quite startling in a new-born baby. He was round and fat and straight-limbed — a splendid baby. Everybody was proud of him, especially his happy father and mother, the King and Queen of Nomansland, who had waited for him all these ten years of their reign.

The only person who was not quite happy about the arrival of the little Prince was the King's brother, who would have been king one day if the baby had not been born. The King was a little sorry for his brother, and gave him a dukedom, and the title of Crown Prince.

The christening was to be a grand affair, with great feasts and ceremonies. The palace was gay with preparations. Four and twenty important people were chosen to be the baby's godfathers and god-mothers. Each would give the little Prince a name. Then, when he came of age, he himself would choose which name and which god-father or godmother he wished to have for the rest of his life.

The christening-day came at last, and it was as lovely as the Prince himself. All the people in the palace were elegantly dressed in new clothes, from the ladies-in-waiting down to the little kitchen-maid. When the Prince was dressed in his magnificent christening robe, he was carried in to be looked at by the Queen, his mother, who had not been able to leave her bed since his birth. She kissed her baby and blessed him.

"I hope he will be good," she said with a gentle smile.

Then she said nothing more to anybody, but turned her face to the window from which she could see the tops of the distant moun-

tains — the "Beautiful Mountains" they were called — where she was born. For many years now she had not been in good health, but she was a sweet and uncomplaining Queen. Her name was Dolorez.

The christening procession was magnificent. All the great and notable persons in the country were there. The four-and-twenty godfathers and godmothers each kissed the baby and pronounced the names each was giving him. Six heralds shouted the names.

Everyone was so busy admiring all this that no one seems to have noticed a slight accident to the Prince. The baby was being carried by a young lady of rank — not his ordinary nursemaid. That young lady had been so busy arranging her train with one hand while she held the baby with the other that she had let him fall at the foot of the marble staircase. She had picked him up so quickly that nobody

41

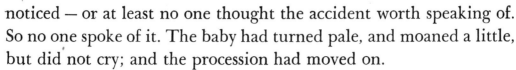

noticed — or at least no one thought the accident worth speaking of. So no one spoke of it. The baby had turned pale, and moaned a little, but did not cry; and the procession had moved on.

The scene was very beautiful. The sun shone through the chapel windows as they stood, the King and his train on one side, the Prince and his attendants on the other.

"It is just like fairyland," whispered one of the little flower girls to another. "The only thing the Prince needs is a fairy godmother."

"Does he?" said a high, soft voice from somewhere. And there, among the children, was somebody, not a child but no bigger than a child, who certainly had not been invited, for she had on no christening clothes. She was a little old woman in a filmy gray gown and gray hooded cloak. Her eyes were gray and so was her hair, but her smile was sweet and childlike.

"Take care," she said to the young lady nurse. "Don't let the baby fall again."

That grand young lady flushed angrily and said sharply:

"Old woman, you will be kind enough not to say 'the baby' but 'the Prince.' Keep away, please!"

"I must kiss him. I am his godmother."

With that the little old woman stretched herself on tiptoe with the help of her stick, and gave the little Prince three kisses.

"This is intolerable," cried the young lady. "Take yourself out of the way, old woman, or the King shall be informed."

"The King does not know me," the old woman replied. "But I know the Queen well. I love her and her child. And, since you dropped him on the marble stairs, I choose to take him for my own. I am his godmother, ready to help him whenever he wants me."

Then, kissing the baby solemnly on the forehead, she said:

"Be called by a new name: Prince Dolor, in memory of your mother, Dolorez."

" 'In memory of'!" Everybody started at the ominous words. And at that moment the great bell of the palace — the bell that was heard only when a death occurred in the Royal family — began to

toll. They listened horror-stricken while the bell tolled twenty-nine times — just the Queen's age. Her Majesty was dead! And when the little Prince was carried back to his mother's room, there was no mother to kiss him. As for his godmother — the little old lady in gray — she seemed to have melted away into thin air, nobody knew when or where. And nobody ever thought about her. But afterwards, by a curious coincidence, the King desired that his son be called by the name of Dolor, after his mother Dolorez.

Everybody was kind to the little Prince. But somehow, after his mother died, everything seemed to go wrong with him. He became sickly and pale, and almost seemed to have stopped growing. After his christening day his legs, which had been so fat and strong, withered and shrank. When he was a year old and his nurse tried to make him stand, he only tumbled down.

Then the people began to talk. What a dreadful misfortune for the country—to have a Prince not able to stand! Even when his health revived, and his cheeks were rosy, and the rest of his body grew larger and stronger, they continued to whisper and shake their heads. Something was not quite right with the poor little Prince.

Of course, nobody told this to the King, his father, for his Majesty was too sad or ill to pay much attention to the child. And it was not long before the King, too, died. Now the little Prince became King of Nomansland. His uncle, the Crown Prince, was named Regent until the little King should come of age. The uncle soon had his wife and her seven sons installed in the palace, where they lived royally and gave splendid entertainments, so that soon everybody shouted, "Long live the Crown Prince!"

No one thought of the little Prince as King, though everyone felt sorry for him, with his grave, sweet face, and his brave way of dragging his body around as he played happily on the floor with his toys. His uncle saw their pity, and he was not pleased. Therefore he made a bold plan. He informed the ministers of the country that the young King was in failing health, and that it would be advisable to send him for a time to the Beautiful Mountains.

The Prince was sent away in great state, with a guard of honor. But soon the nation was told that the poor little Prince died on the road. His coffin was brought back and buried with great pomp and ceremony. So Prince Dolor was seen no more. The country went into deep mourning for him and then forgot him, and his uncle became King in his stead.

And what of the little lame Prince, who had been so quickly forgotten?

Beyond the mountains, between them and the sea, lay a barren strip of land. It had neither a tree nor a bush—not a resting place for bird or beast was on that desolate plain. It was not a pleasant place to live, and nobody did live there, apparently. The only sign that anyone had even been there was one large round tower which rose up a hundred feet high in the very center of the plain. It was solidly built of brick, and had no doors or windows, except that near the top one could see slits in the wall. On its very top, but concealed from view by a parapet, was a skylight.

One winter night, when all the plain was white with moonlight, there was seen crossing it a great black horse, ridden by a man who was also big and black and carrying before him on the saddle a woman and a child. The woman had a sad, fierce look, and no wonder,

for she was a criminal under sentence of death. But her sentence had been changed to one almost as dreadful: she was to live in the lonely tower with the child, and was allowed to live as long as the child lived—no longer. This, in order that she would take good care of him, for those who put him there were equally afraid of his dying and of his living. Yet he was only a little gentle boy, very helpless with his small shriveled legs which could neither stand nor run away. For the little boy was Prince Dolor.

When they reached the foot of the tower, there was light enough for them to see a huge chain dangling from the parapet halfway to the ground. The man took from his saddle the pieces of a ladder, fitted it together, and lifted it up to meet the chain. Then he mounted to the top of the tower, and slung from it a sort of chair in which the woman and the child placed themselves and were drawn up. The man then descended the ladder, disassembled the pieces and packed them in his saddle-bag, mounted his horse, and disappeared across the plain.

Every month he returned, bringing provisions and toys and books. He always saw the young Prince, to make sure he was alive, and then went away until the following month. He was deaf and dumb, so could neither tell nor repeat anything.

While his childhood lasted, Prince Dolor was happy enough. His nurse was kind to him, and he had everything he needed—except love, which he had never known and therefore did not miss. He played about in the four rooms of the luxurious apartment, learned to crawl like a fly and to jump like a frog, and to run about on all fours like a puppy. He did not know he was not like other boys, for he had never seen a boy. He did not pity himself at all.

By and by he began to learn lessons which his nurse taught him, partly to amuse herself. She was not a stupid woman, and the Prince was not stupid either, so they got on well, and he learned quickly. Soon he could read easily, and he took to books, which the deaf-mute brought him. From this time a change came over the boy. He began to ask questions of his nurse; but she had been forbidden, on pain of

45

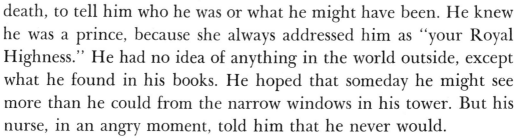

death, to tell him who he was or what he might have been. He knew he was a prince, because she always addressed him as "your Royal Highness." He had no idea of anything in the world outside, except what he found in his books. He hoped that someday he might see more than he could from the narrow windows in his tower. But his nurse, in an angry moment, told him that he never would.

One day, as he was sitting, sad and lonely, at the window slit in his room, he cried aloud:

"I wish I had somebody to tell me all about it—about many things. I wish I had a person who would be fond of me. Oh, I want somebody—dreadfully, dreadfully!"

As he spoke there sounded behind him a slight tap-tap-tap, as of a stick or cane. Twisting himself around, Prince Dolor saw a little old woman. Her hair was gray and her dress was gray, and there was a gray shadow over her wherever she moved.

"My own little boy," she said, in a sweet tender voice, "I could not come to you until you said you wanted me, but now you do want me, so here I am."

"Are you my mother?" asked the Prince. For he knew that little boys in his books had mothers, and he had often wondered what had become of his own.

"No," said the visitor, with a half-sad smile, "but your mother was a dear friend of mine. I am your godmother."

"I like you very much," cried the little Prince. "Promise me that you will never go away."

"I must. But I will leave a present behind me—something that will take you wherever you want to go, and show you all you wish to see."

"What is it?"

"A traveling-cloak."

The Prince's face fell. "I don't want a cloak, for I never go out. Sometimes Nurse carries me around the parapet, but that is all. I can't walk, you know, as she does."

"The more reason why you should ride; and besides——"

Just then they heard the nurse outside the door; she was bringing him his dinner. The Prince was frightened. What would she say when she saw his godmother? He need not have worried, for as she entered the door he looked around and saw there was no one else there. His lovely godmother had melted away like the rainbow out of the sky.

"What's this rubbish?" said the nurse crossly, kicking aside a little bundle that lay beside the Prince on the floor.

"Oh, nothing!" cried the Prince, darting after it. He pushed it quickly into his pocket, thinking it must be something belonging to his dear, kind godmother. It was, though he did not know it, his wonderful traveling-cloak.

As soon as he was alone again, the Prince took out his treasure to examine it. It had dwindled down to a size that could easily fit into his pocket. When he opened it, he found it to be a mere piece of cloth, of a dark green color and very worn and shabby. It did not look like a treasure at all. He could not imagine what he was intended to do with it, since he had no need for out-door clothes. However, because it was a gift from his godmother, he folded it carefully and hid it away where his nurse would not find it. There he left it and almost forgot about it.

Then, one day, the Prince fell ill. As he was lying in his bed, bored and lonely, he began to think how nice it would be, since he could not walk, to be able to fly like a bird. Then he thought of his godmother, and said aloud:

"Godmother, dear, have you quite forgotten me?"

He felt a light kiss, and found himself nestled in his godmother's arms. At once he felt well and strong again.

"Dear Godmother, I am so very lonely. I wish I could leave here."

"Where is your traveling-cloak?" she asked.

He told her he had hidden it away.

"Take it out," she said, "and shake out the dust. Then spread it on the floor. Wait till the edges turn up like a rim all round.

Then, after you have opened the skylight, set yourself down in the middle of the cloak like a frog on a water-lily leaf, say 'Abracadabra, dum, dum, dum,' and—see what happens!"

The Prince laughed ,and wondered how a wise old woman like his godmother could talk such nonsense.

"It doesn't matter whether you believe me or not," said she. "But when you want to go traveling, do as I have told you. And when you want to come back again, say 'Abracadabra, tum, tum, ti.' That's all. Goodby." A puff of pleasant air passed by him, and she was gone.

That night the Prince could hardly wait until his nurse had cleared away his supper tray and left him alone. Then he fetched the cloak. He started to untie the knots that bound it together, and then it began to unfold itself. It laid itself down on the carpet, and the rim turned up all round till it was breast high. Meanwhile the cloak had grown until it was quite large enough for one person to sit in as comfortably as in a boat. For a moment the Prince looked at it with some hesitation. Then, gathering courage, he said to himself, "Here I go!"

He sprang right into the middle of the cloak, squatted down with his arms wrapped tight around his knees, and, still only half-believing, repeated the words, "Abracadabra, dum, dum, dum!"

For a moment nothing happened. Then the cloak rose, slowly and steadily, higher and higher, until it paused just beneath the skylight. Remembering his godmother's instructions, the Prince pushed open the bolt which held the glass, and the cloak carried him up and out into the clear fresh air, with the sky above him and the earth below.

The Prince had never felt any such delicious sensation before! When the stars came out—so many of them—he tried to count them. But after a while he became bewildered, and in the cool breezes he began to feel chilled. He thought he had better go home. But how? In the excitement he had forgotten the other words his godmother had told him. As the cloak began to whirl faster and faster, he became frightened.

"Dear Godmother," he cried, "do help me. Tell me just this once, and I'll never forget again!"

Instantly the words came into his head: "Abracadabra, tum, tum, ti!" The cloak turned slowly and started back. The Prince slid in through the open skylight just in time, for his nurse came in just then to see why he was sitting in the dark. As she shut the skylight with a bang, the cloak had folded itself into a small ball and rolled into a corner where she could not see it.

She left the room grumbling, and the Prince thought:

"Poor woman! *She* hasn't got a traveling-cloak."

This was the first of many wonderful journeys the Prince made on his traveling-cloak. He saw many things in the wide world that made him happy: flowers and trees and people. He saw some things that made him sad, as when he saw a little boy about his own age running freely as he knew he could never run. One day, riding on his cloak, he found on his eyes a pair of spectacles to help him see better the flowers and other growing things on the ground. For these he called aloud his thanks to his godmother. Another time she pro-

49

vided him with a pair of silver ears to place on his own, that he might hear the sounds beneath him as he flew over fields and villages. When he was cold, he had but to wish, and found a warm robe wrapped softly around him; when he was hungry, he found a packet of delicious food in his pocket; when he was thirsty, a large glass vessel he had never noticed before caught the raindrops and provided a refreshing drink.

One day, as he rode on his cloak lost in thought, he heard the song of a skylark. Peering over the side, he saw the tiny brown bird coming nearer and nearer until finally it perched on his shoulder. He held it gently in his hands for a while, and it seemed content there. But as he came near to the tower, he could not bear the thought of imprisoning the lovely bird, and he opened his hands and let it fly away. But the lark did not go far; it kept hovering about the tower, and he heard it singing still. All through the winter months it stayed and sang to him.

Prince Dolor was now quite a big boy—not tall, but strong and manly. He began to wonder about the work men do. What would be his work? He knew he was a prince, and he had read in his books that princes became kings. One day he said to his nurse:

"Dear nurse, tell me—what is a king? Shall I ever be one?"

So long a time had passed since she had been threatened into silence, and the years of close imprisonment had so softened her feelings toward the young Prince, that the woman now considered for a moment. Would her oath "not to say a word" be broken if she wrote with a pencil what was to be "told"? She knew this was a mere quibble—but still she felt a great desire to do it. So she wrote on the Prince's slate, ready to rub out the writing in a minute, these words: "You are a king."

Then she wrote down, in a few hurried sentences, his history —how his parents had died and his uncle had usurped his throne and sent him to end his days in this lonely tower.

"I, too," she added, bursting into tears. "Unless, indeed, you could get out into the world and fight for your rights like a man."

That night the Prince scarcely slept. He barely listened to his little lark singing, for things more serious and important had taken possession of his mind. Should he do as his nurse had said? And what was there he could do, with his helpless body?

"Godmother, help me!" he cried.

There was no answer, only the little lark outside the window sang louder as the sun rose, flooding the room with light.

Prince Dolor sprang out of bed and began dressing himself, which was hard work, for he had always depended on his nurse to do this.

"But now I must learn to be independent," he thought. "Imagine a king being dressed by a nurse!"

He spread his traveling-cloak, jumped into the middle of it, said the magic words and was through the skylight immediately.

"Goodby, pretty lark!" he shouted. "You have been my pleasure; now I must go and work."

But suddenly he remembered that he did not know where to go. Again he begged his godmother to take him where he ought to go and show him what he ought to see. For this journey was not for pleasure.

The cloak was traveling now faster than he had ever known it to do—over land and mountains, cloud-land and great shoreless lakes. After some time he heard a murmur which grew like the hum of a giant hive of bees. Stretching his chin over the rim of his cloak, Prince Dolor saw and heard, for the first time, the life of a great city. He was puzzled and bewildered.

"I don't understand it, and there is nobody to tell me. I wish I had somebody to speak to."

"Do you? Then please speak to me." The voice that squeaked this reply came from a bird, a great black-and-white creature that flew into the cloak. "My name is Mag," she told him. "I am a magpie."

As they sailed on she showed him many objects of interest. When he asked about them she said:

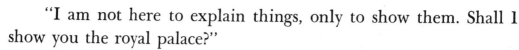

"I am not here to explain things, only to show them. Shall I show you the royal palace?"

She showed him the magnificent palace, its terraces and gardens, its battlements and towers. Suddenly Prince Dolor said:

"I should like to see the King."

"Ah," said the magpie, "the King is ill, though he does not wish it to be generally known. But perhaps you might take a look at him in a way I often do."

As she spoke she flew down to the palace roof, where the cloak had come to rest. Pecking at the tile with her beak, she made a little hole, uncovering a sort of door through which a room below could be seen.

"Kneel down and take a peep at his Majesty," she told him. "Be quick, for I must soon close it up again."

For a moment the Prince hesitated. Would it be rude, he wondered? But he was so excited at the thought of seeing the King, his uncle who had dethroned him, that he could not resist.

The Prince gazed eagerly down into an enormous room which was furnished more luxuriously than any he could ever have imagined. The room was very quiet and he could see no one.

"Where is the King?" asked the boy, puzzled.

"There," said Mag, pointing with her claw to a magnificent bed. In the center of it lay a small figure, quite straight and still. The eyes were closed.

"Is that the King?" whispered Prince Dolor.

"Yes," replied the bird.

"What is the matter with him?" asked the Prince.

"He is dead," said the magpie.

The Prince found his anger at his wicked uncle melting away. The still figure looked so helpless. So this was what being "dead" meant? And even kings died?

Quickly now the magpie shut the little door in the tiles. The Prince, sitting in the center of his traveling-cloak, was silent and thoughtful.

"Come," said Mag, "we will go and see the fun—at a safe distance, though. Now that the King is dead, there will be a revolution."

And sure enough, as soon as the bell began to toll and the guns to fire, announcing to the kingdom that it was without a king, the people gathered in crowds. The murmur rose into a shout and the shout into a roar. "The King is dead! Down with the crown! Hurrah for no government at all!'' And then began such a hideous scene of fighting and shooting and killing that the gentle Prince Dolor could hardly bear it. Stopping his ears and shutting his eyes, he cried at last:

"Oh, let me go home!"

"Goodby, then," said the magpie. "We may meet again some time."

As she looked at him the Prince thought her eyes changed to human eyes—the eyes of his godmother. But she quickly spread her wings and flew away. Prince Dolor, sick and miserable, fell into a kind of swoon. When he awoke he found himself back in his own room, with the light of early dawn coming in at the windows.

When he sat up in bed, he was surprised to find that his nurse had not come in to tidy up. The dust lay thick on chairs and tables. He called to his nurse, but there was no answer. Springing out of bed, he crept on his knees from room to room. He was completely alone. What could have happened? Looking down from the window, he noticed the prints of a horse's hoofs in the mud below. That was it, then! The deaf-mute had come and taken the nurse away to freedom. How glad she must have been to go! But how cruel to leave him there, helpless and alone!

Somehow he must manage for himself. He did the best he could, dragging himself through five lonely days. But now he was near the end of his provisions. What would happen now? Must he die before he had a chance to do something worth doing?

Sitting dolefully by his window he thought he heard a faint sound. He listened intently. Yes, it *was* something, and it was coming nearer. It was the sound of a trumpet. For his nurse had not been so cruel after all, and had done a very heroic thing. As soon as she had learned that the King was dead, a daring idea came into her head. She persuaded the deaf-mute to take her with him, and they galloped like the wind from city to city, spreading everywhere the news that Prince Dolor, the rightful King, was alive and well, the noblest young Prince that ever was born. And the people, weary of the harsh rule of their late King, but equally weary of the horrors of the past few

days, eagerly grasped at the idea of having for their monarch the son of the beloved Queen Dolorez.

"Let Prince Dolor be our King," they shouted. They denounced the late King as a usurper, turned his family out of the palace, and went with great rejoicing to fetch their new sovereign, traveling in solemn procession to Hopeless Tower.

There they found the young Prince sitting on the floor. They knelt before him and offered him the crown on a velvet cushion. Small though he was and lame (which the courtiers pretended not to notice) such a glow came into his face and such dignity into his demeanor that he became kinglike.

"Yes," he said. "If you desire it I will be your King. And I will do my best to make my people happy. But you, my lords, must help, for I am only a little boy still."

"Not so little," was the respectful answer. "We have searched the records and find that Your Majesty is precisely fifteen years old."

"Am I?" said Prince Dolor, and his first thought was that now he should have a birthday, with a whole nation to celebrate it. But then he remembered that his childish days were done. He was a monarch now. Even his nurse, to whom he had held out his hand, had kissed it reverently and called him "Your Majesty the King."

"A king must always be a king, I suppose," he thought, half-sadly, as, left alone for a few moments, he put off his boy's clothes and put on magnificent robes, ready to be conveyed to the royal palace. Now the trumpets blew louder, and the people shouted for their new King. And so Prince Dolor quitted the tower which he had entered so sadly as a little helpless baby—quitted it as the great King of Nomansland.

The only thing he took away with him was a tiny bundle which was so small that the lords and gentlemen and soldiers who escorted him with such triumphant splendor couldn't have noticed it. Or, if they had, they might have mistaken it for a bit of flannel or an old pocket-handkerchief.

It was his traveling-cloak.

THE SLEEPING BEAUTY 57

The Sleeping Beauty

ILLUSTRATED BY GRACE CLARKE

ONCE UPON A TIME in a kingdom not too near and not too far, there lived a King and Queen who had everything in the world they wanted, except the one thing they wished for most. They had no children, and they longed to have a son or a daughter.

One day, as the Queen was sitting by the side of the lake lost in sad thoughts, a tiny fairy rose up from the water and gave her a white flower. "Take this," said the fairy, "and your dearest wish will be fulfilled."

The Queen was overjoyed when at last a beautiful baby daughter was born to her. The King was so delighted that he ordered a great christening feast be held, the like of which had never been seen before.

Messengers were sent out to invite all the fairies in the kingdom to be godmothers to the Princess. Six good fairies were found, and they all came to honor the royal baby.

The christening took place with great pomp and splendor. After the christening the guests returned to the castle for the royal banquet. Before each fairy was placed a plate, knife, and spoon of pure gold. But just as they were about to sit down at the banquet table an unexpected guest appeared, her untidy clothes all rusty black. She was an old and ugly fairy who had not been invited because the messengers had not known where to find her. The King ordered another place to be set for her, but as he had no more golden dishes and spoons, hers had to be ordinary ones. At this she became very angry, feeling that she was not being as well treated as the others, and one of the younger fairies heard her muttering angry threats. When the banquet was over, the young fairy, fearing that the Black Fairy would try to harm the Princess; hid herself behind the curtains to be ready to help if need be.

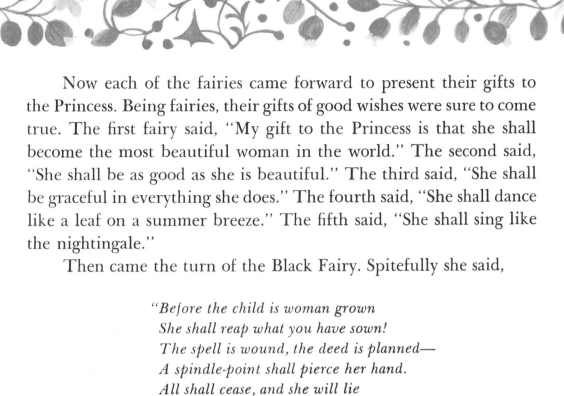

Now each of the fairies came forward to present their gifts to the Princess. Being fairies, their gifts of good wishes were sure to come true. The first fairy said, "My gift to the Princess is that she shall become the most beautiful woman in the world." The second said, "She shall be as good as she is beautiful." The third said, "She shall be graceful in everything she does." The fourth said, "She shall dance like a leaf on a summer breeze." The fifth said, "She shall sing like the nightingale."

Then came the turn of the Black Fairy. Spitefully she said,

> *"Before the child is woman grown*
> *She shall reap what you have sown!*
> *The spell is wound, the deed is planned—*
> *A spindle-point shall pierce her hand.*
> *All shall cease, and she will lie*
> *Deep in sleep until she die."*

The King and Queen were almost beside themselves with grief.
But now the young fairy who had hidden behind the curtains flew to the side of the Princess's cradle, and said:

"O King and Queen, do not weep! I cannot entirely undo the evil wished by the old fairy, but the Princess shall not die. For here is my gift to her:

> *"Safe from passion, safe from strife*
> *Safe from all that threatens life*
> *None shall touch her, naught shall shake her*
> *Till a true Prince comes to wake her."*

Now the King did everything in his power to prevent the misfortune foretold by the Black Fairy. He commanded that no one in the whole kingdom, on pain of death, should spin with a spindle. All the spinning wheels in the kingdom were to be burned.

In time the little Princess grew into a beautiful young girl, and all the good wishes of the fairies came true. Great care was taken that she should never know of such a thing as a spinning wheel.

One evening when she was just fifteen years old she was alone in her room, preparing to go to bed. Suddenly she thought she heard a strange whirring sound. Opening her door, she followed the sound which seemed to come from far above her. After climbing many stairs, she came to the top of a tall tower. A door opened into a small

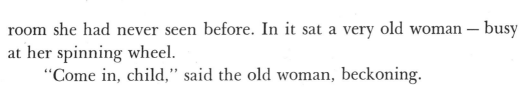

room she had never seen before. In it sat a very old woman — busy at her spinning wheel.

"Come in, child," said the old woman, beckoning.

"What are you doing, Granny?" asked the Princess.

"I'm spinning, my pretty child," said the woman.

For a moment the Princess watched, fascinated. Then she said: "Let me see if I can do it."

As she said this she picked up the spindle, and then—the point of the spindle pierced her finger. At once she fell into a deep sleep.

At this same moment everything ceased to move in the palace and everyone fell asleep. The King and Queen, dressing in their rooms, fell asleep at once, and with them the courtiers, the pages, the footmen, and all the servants. The cook, who was just about to box the kitchen boy's ears because he had made a mistake, fell asleep, and the boy did too. The horses went to sleep in the stable, the cock in the yard, the doves on the roof, and the flies on the wall.

61

All around the castle, there now grew up a hedge of briars and thorns so tough and thick that it seemed as if no one could ever get through it. Nothing could be seen of the castle but the high tower where the lovely Princess slept.

From time to time princes in far countries heard of the Sleeping Beauty. The story was told by fathers to sons, and by sons to their sons. Many tried to reach the castle, but none could get through the thorny hedge, and many perished in the wild jungle that had grown up there.

At last just a hundred years had passed. On that very day a king's son came riding through the land, and when he heard the story of the Sleeping Beauty, he vowed that he would awaken her. As he came to the thorny hedge, the branches gave way and let him pass. The gates, overgrown with briars, swung open as he approached. When he entered the courtyard, what a sight met his eyes! The cock was asleep, and so were the horses in their stalls, and the doves that perched, with heads under their wings, on the roof. In the kitchen the cook was asleep, with his hand raised as if to strike the sleeping kitchen boy beside him. All the guards about the castle slept quietly, and in the royal chambers the King and Queen and all the ladies and gentlemen of the court were asleep, caught in the very posture of what they were doing so long ago.

At last the Prince reached the tower where the Princess slept. Eagerly he opened the door of the little room. There lay the Princess, as fresh and lovely as on the day she fell asleep. The Prince bent down and gently kissed her. She opened her eyes and smiled. "Is it you, Prince?" she murmured; "I have waited for you a long time."

And now the whole castle awoke. The King and Queen and all their attendants rubbed their eyes and looked about them. The horses in the stable got up and shook themselves. The cock began to crow. The doves on the roof lifted their heads from under their wings and began to coo. The royal standard on its pole waved in the breeze. The flies on the wall began to crawl again. In the kitchen the cook boxed the boy's ears so hard that he cried out. The fire on the hearth blazed up, and the meat went on roasting.

Hand in hand the Prince and Princess went down the tower stairs. Very soon their wedding was celebrated with all splendor, and they lived long and happily together.

DICK WHITTINGTON AND HIS CAT 65

Dick Whittington and His Cat

ILLUSTRATED BY FRED BANBERY

IN THE REIGN of the famous King Edward III there was a little boy called Dick Whittington, whose father and mother died when he was very young. As poor Dick was not old enough to work, he was very badly off; he got but little for his dinner, and sometimes nothing at all for his breakfast; for the people who lived in the village were very poor indeed, and could not spare him much more than the parings of potatoes, and now and then a hard crust of bread.

Now Dick had heard many, many very strange things about the great city called London; for the country people at that time thought that folks in London were all fine gentlemen and ladies, and that there was singing and music there all day long, and that the streets were all paved with gold.

One day a large wagon and eight horses, all with bells at their heads, drove through the village while Dick was standing by the signpost. He thought that this wagon must be going to the fine town of London; so he took courage, and asked the wagoner to let him walk with him by the side of the wagon. As soon as the wagoner heard that poor Dick had no father or mother, and saw by his ragged clothes that he could not be worse off than he was, he told him he might go with him, so they set off together.

Dick got safely to London, and was in such a hurry to see the fine streets paved all over with gold that he did not even stay to thank the kind wagoner. He ran off as fast as his legs could carry him.

66

Poor Dick ran till he was tired, and had quite forgot his friend the wagoner; but at last, finding that it was growing dark, and that every way he turned he saw nothing but dirt instead of gold, he sat down in a dark corner and cried himself to sleep.

Dick was all night in the streets; and the next morning, being very hungry, he got up and walked about.

A butcher shop nearby attracted his attention and he went over to it and rapped confidently on the door. It was opened by the butcher, holding a cleaver in one hand and a piece of meat in the other.

"Please, sir, I'd like a position," Dick said.

The butcher slammed the door in his face.

Less confidently this time, Dick rapped on the door of a tailor shop. Here too he met with no success.

Tired and dejected, he went on, and the next place he tried was the White Swan Tavern. A man with a goblet in his hands opened the door and asked what the boy wanted.

"Please, sir," said Dick, "if I could work . . . anything . . . for a bite of food . . ."

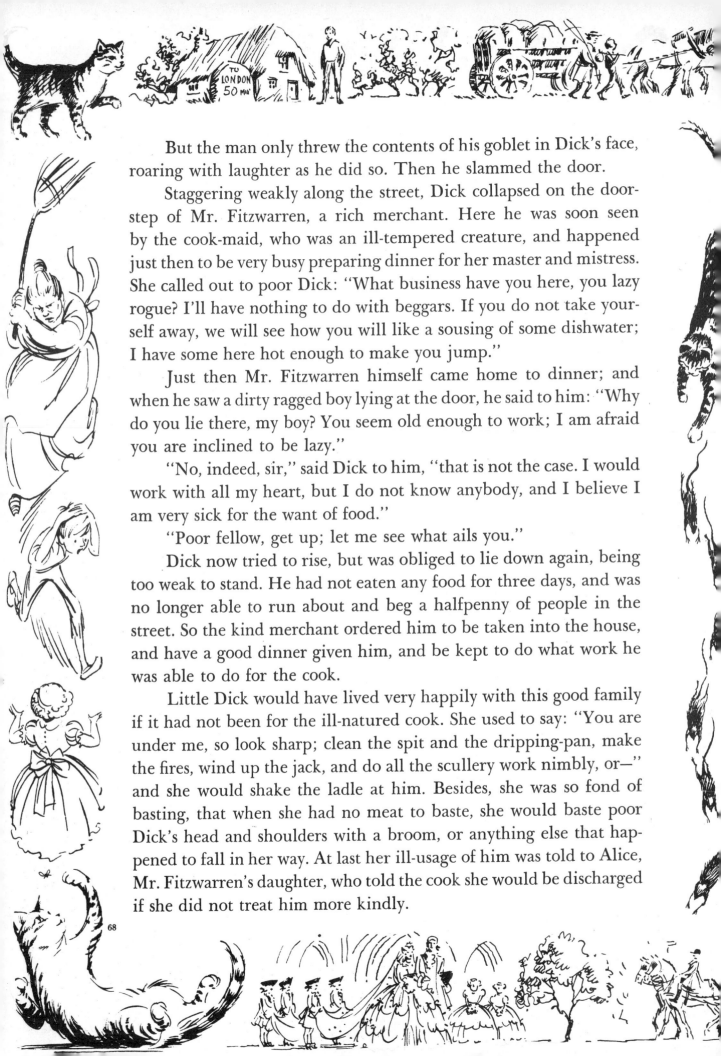

But the man only threw the contents of his goblet in Dick's face, roaring with laughter as he did so. Then he slammed the door.

Staggering weakly along the street, Dick collapsed on the door-step of Mr. Fitzwarren, a rich merchant. Here he was soon seen by the cook-maid, who was an ill-tempered creature, and happened just then to be very busy preparing dinner for her master and mistress. She called out to poor Dick: "What business have you here, you lazy rogue? I'll have nothing to do with beggars. If you do not take your-self away, we will see how you will like a sousing of some dishwater; I have some here hot enough to make you jump."

Just then Mr. Fitzwarren himself came home to dinner; and when he saw a dirty ragged boy lying at the door, he said to him: "Why do you lie there, my boy? You seem old enough to work; I am afraid you are inclined to be lazy."

"No, indeed, sir," said Dick to him, "that is not the case. I would work with all my heart, but I do not know anybody, and I believe I am very sick for the want of food."

"Poor fellow, get up; let me see what ails you."

Dick now tried to rise, but was obliged to lie down again, being too weak to stand. He had not eaten any food for three days, and was no longer able to run about and beg a halfpenny of people in the street. So the kind merchant ordered him to be taken into the house, and have a good dinner given him, and be kept to do what work he was able to do for the cook.

Little Dick would have lived very happily with this good family if it had not been for the ill-natured cook. She used to say: "You are under me, so look sharp; clean the spit and the dripping-pan, make the fires, wind up the jack, and do all the scullery work nimbly, or—" and she would shake the ladle at him. Besides, she was so fond of basting, that when she had no meat to baste, she would baste poor Dick's head and shoulders with a broom, or anything else that hap-pened to fall in her way. At last her ill-usage of him was told to Alice, Mr. Fitzwarren's daughter, who told the cook she would be discharged if she did not treat him more kindly.

68

The cook behaved better after that. And when a whole year had gone by, Dick was given his wages—a penny—the first he had ever earned.

But now Dick had another hardship to get over. His bed stood in a garret, where there were so many holes in the floor and the walls that every night he was tormented with rats and mice.

One day he was strolling along the street when he ran into a hubbub. A door flew open and a man appeared carrying a cat. As he brushed past Dick he said, "Out of my way, boy! Puss here is due for a swim."

"I beg your pardon, sir," said Dick, "but I never knew a cat that could swim. . . . Oh, do you mean you are going to drown it? What a cruel thing to do! I beg you not to."

"And why shouldn't I?" the man asked angrily.

Dick continued his pleading. At last the man said, "If you're so keen on keeping this cat alive why don't you buy her?" So Dick did, paying for the cat with his only penny. And as he took the cat he whispered to her, "Now you are my fortune."

Dick hid his cat in the garret, and always took care to carry a part of his dinner to her; and in a short time he had no more trouble with the rats and mice, but slept quite soundly every night.

69

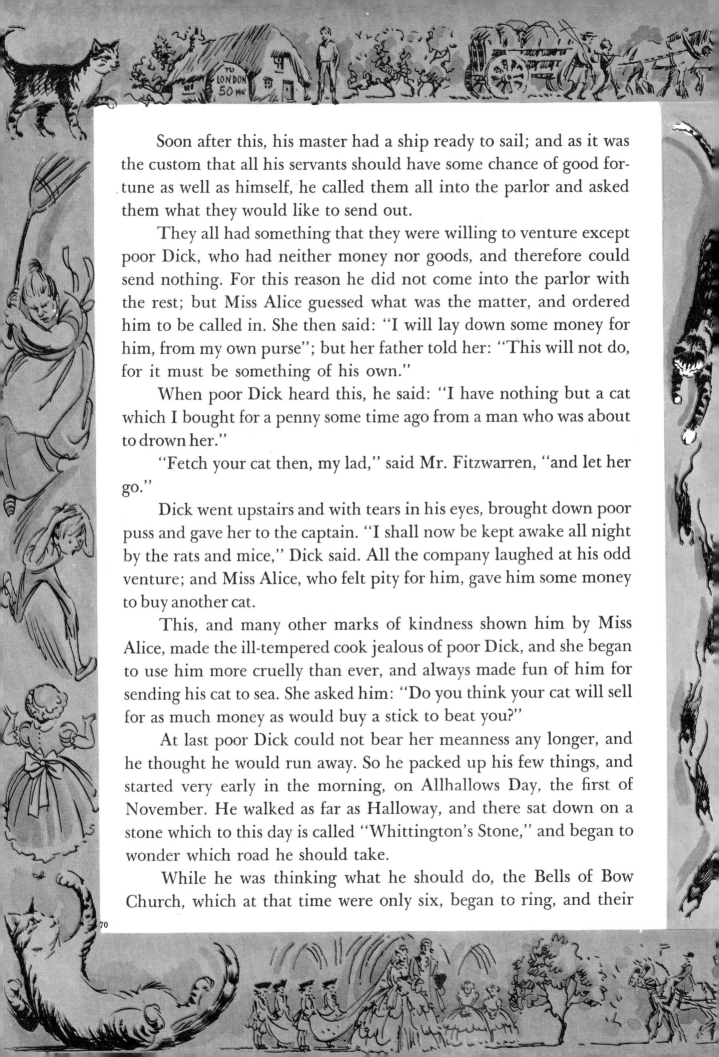

Soon after this, his master had a ship ready to sail; and as it was the custom that all his servants should have some chance of good fortune as well as himself, he called them all into the parlor and asked them what they would like to send out.

They all had something that they were willing to venture except poor Dick, who had neither money nor goods, and therefore could send nothing. For this reason he did not come into the parlor with the rest; but Miss Alice guessed what was the matter, and ordered him to be called in. She then said: "I will lay down some money for him, from my own purse"; but her father told her: "This will not do, for it must be something of his own."

When poor Dick heard this, he said: "I have nothing but a cat which I bought for a penny some time ago from a man who was about to drown her."

"Fetch your cat then, my lad," said Mr. Fitzwarren, "and let her go."

Dick went upstairs and with tears in his eyes, brought down poor puss and gave her to the captain. "I shall now be kept awake all night by the rats and mice," Dick said. All the company laughed at his odd venture; and Miss Alice, who felt pity for him, gave him some money to buy another cat.

This, and many other marks of kindness shown him by Miss Alice, made the ill-tempered cook jealous of poor Dick, and she began to use him more cruelly than ever, and always made fun of him for sending his cat to sea. She asked him: "Do you think your cat will sell for as much money as would buy a stick to beat you?"

At last poor Dick could not bear her meanness any longer, and he thought he would run away. So he packed up his few things, and started very early in the morning, on Allhallows Day, the first of November. He walked as far as Halloway, and there sat down on a stone which to this day is called "Whittington's Stone," and began to wonder which road he should take.

While he was thinking what he should do, the Bells of Bow Church, which at that time were only six, began to ring, and their

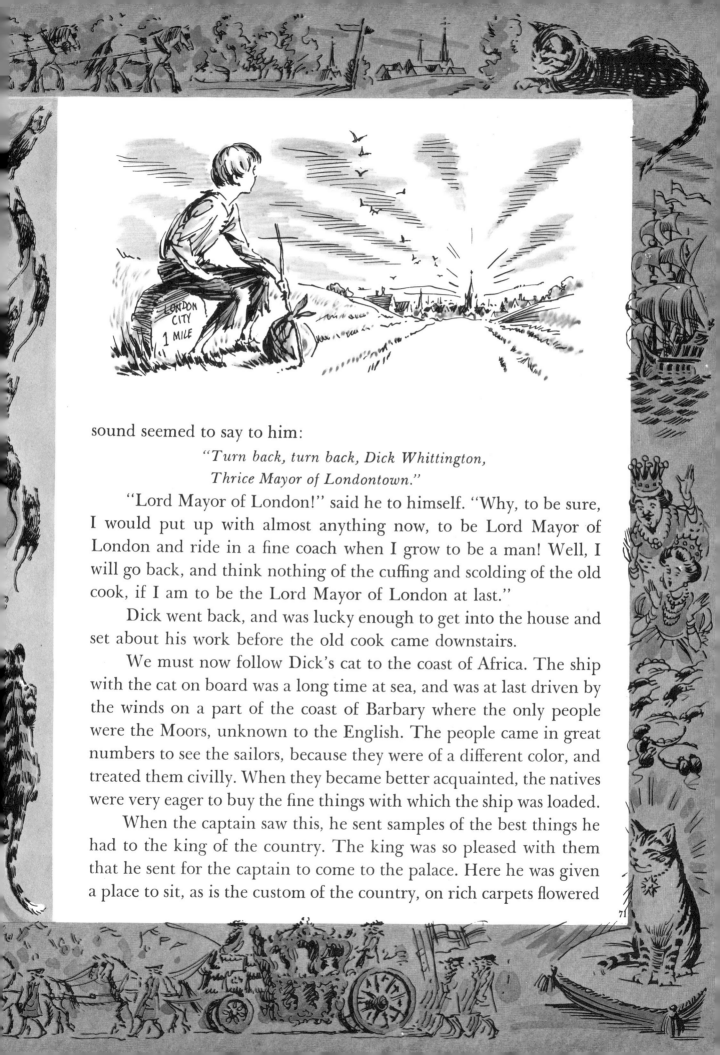

sound seemed to say to him:

"*Turn back, turn back, Dick Whittington,*
Thrice Mayor of Londontown."

"Lord Mayor of London!" said he to himself. "Why, to be sure, I would put up with almost anything now, to be Lord Mayor of London and ride in a fine coach when I grow to be a man! Well, I will go back, and think nothing of the cuffing and scolding of the old cook, if I am to be the Lord Mayor of London at last."

Dick went back, and was lucky enough to get into the house and set about his work before the old cook came downstairs.

We must now follow Dick's cat to the coast of Africa. The ship with the cat on board was a long time at sea, and was at last driven by the winds on a part of the coast of Barbary where the only people were the Moors, unknown to the English. The people came in great numbers to see the sailors, because they were of a different color, and treated them civilly. When they became better acquainted, the natives were very eager to buy the fine things with which the ship was loaded.

When the captain saw this, he sent samples of the best things he had to the king of the country. The king was so pleased with them that he sent for the captain to come to the palace. Here he was given a place to sit, as is the custom of the country, on rich carpets flowered

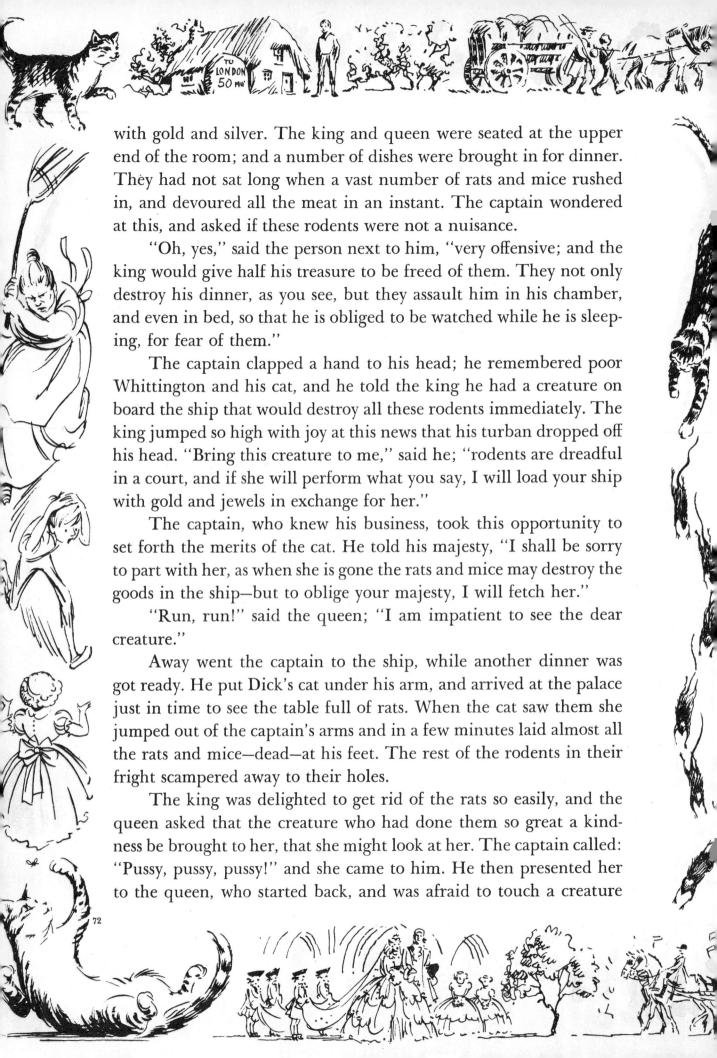

with gold and silver. The king and queen were seated at the upper end of the room; and a number of dishes were brought in for dinner. They had not sat long when a vast number of rats and mice rushed in, and devoured all the meat in an instant. The captain wondered at this, and asked if these rodents were not a nuisance.

"Oh, yes," said the person next to him, "very offensive; and the king would give half his treasure to be freed of them. They not only destroy his dinner, as you see, but they assault him in his chamber, and even in bed, so that he is obliged to be watched while he is sleeping, for fear of them."

The captain clapped a hand to his head; he remembered poor Whittington and his cat, and he told the king he had a creature on board the ship that would destroy all these rodents immediately. The king jumped so high with joy at this news that his turban dropped off his head. "Bring this creature to me," said he; "rodents are dreadful in a court, and if she will perform what you say, I will load your ship with gold and jewels in exchange for her."

The captain, who knew his business, took this opportunity to set forth the merits of the cat. He told his majesty, "I shall be sorry to part with her, as when she is gone the rats and mice may destroy the goods in the ship—but to oblige your majesty, I will fetch her."

"Run, run!" said the queen; "I am impatient to see the dear creature."

Away went the captain to the ship, while another dinner was got ready. He put Dick's cat under his arm, and arrived at the palace just in time to see the table full of rats. When the cat saw them she jumped out of the captain's arms and in a few minutes laid almost all the rats and mice—dead—at his feet. The rest of the rodents in their fright scampered away to their holes.

The king was delighted to get rid of the rats so easily, and the queen asked that the creature who had done them so great a kindness be brought to her, that she might look at her. The captain called: "Pussy, pussy, pussy!" and she came to him. He then presented her to the queen, who started back, and was afraid to touch a creature

who had wrought such havoc among the rats and mice. However, when the captain stroked the cat and called: "Pussy, pussy," the queen also touched her and cried: "Putty, putty," for she had not learned English. The captain then put the cat down on the queen's lap, where she purred and played with her majesty's hand, and then purred herself to sleep.

The king, having seen the cat's exploits, and being informed that her kittens would stock the whole country and keep it free from rats, bargained with the captain for the whole ship's cargo, and then gave him ten times as much for the cat as all the rest was worth.

The captain then took leave of the king and queen, and set sail with a fair wind for England. After a pleasant voyage he arrived safely in London.

Early one morning, Mr. Fitzwarren had just come to his counting-house and seated himself at the desk when there came a tap, tap at the door. "Who's there?" said Mr. Fitzwarren. "A friend," answered the other; "I come to bring you good news of your ship *Unicorn*." The merchant, bustling up in such a hurry that he forgot his gout, opened the door, and whom should he see waiting but the captain and his mate, with a cabinet of jewels and a bill of lading. When he looked at this the merchant lifted up his eyes and thanked Heaven for so prosperous a voyage.

They then told the story of the cat, and showed the rich present that the king and queen had sent to poor Dick. As soon as the merchant heard this, he called out to his servants:

> "Go send him in, and tell him of his fame;
> Pray call him Mr. Whittington by name."

Mr. Fitzwarren now showed himself to be a good man; for when some of his servants said that so great a treasure was too much for the boy, he answered: "God forbid I should deprive him of the value of a single penny; it is his own, and he shall have it to a farthing."

When he sent for Dick, who at that time was scouring pots for the cook, and was quite dirty, the boy wanted to excuse himself from coming into the county-house, saying, "The room is swept, and my shoes are dirty and full of hobnails." But the merchant insisted that he come in.

When Mr. Fitzwarren ordered a chair to be set for him, Dick began to think they were making fun of him, so he said: "Do not play tricks with a poor simple boy. Let me go down again, if you please, to my work."

"Indeed, Mr. Whittington," said the merchant, "we are all quite in earnest with you, and I most heartily rejoice in the news that these gentlemen have brought you. The captain has sold your cat to the King of Barbary, and brought you in return far more riches than I possess in the whole world; and I trust you may long enjoy them!"

Mr. Fitzwarren then told the men to open the great treasure they had brought with them, and said: "Mr. Whittington has nothing to do but to put it in some place of safety."

Poor Dick hardly knew how to behave himself, he was so overcome with joy. He begged his master to take what part of the treasure he pleased, since he owed it all to his kindness. "No, no," answered Mr. Fitzwarren, "this is all your own; and I have no doubt but you will use it well."

Dick next asked his mistress, and then Miss Alice, to accept a part of his good fortune; but they would not, and at the same time told him they felt great joy at his unexpected success. But this poor fellow was too kind-hearted to keep it all to himself; so he made a present to the captain, the mate, and the rest of Mr. Fitzwarren's servants; and even to the ill-natured old cook.

After this Mr. Fitzwarren advised him to send for a proper tailor and get himself dressed like a gentleman. He also told him he was welcome to live in his house till he could provide himself with a better one.

When Whittington's face was washed, his hair curled, his hat cocked, and he was dressed in a good suit of clothes, he was as handsome and genteel as any young man who visited at Mr. Fitzwarren's. As a result, Miss Alice, who had always been kind to him, but thought of him only with pity, now looked upon him as fit to be her sweetheart; and the more so, no doubt, because Whittington was now always thinking what he could do to oblige her, and giving her the prettiest presents he could find.

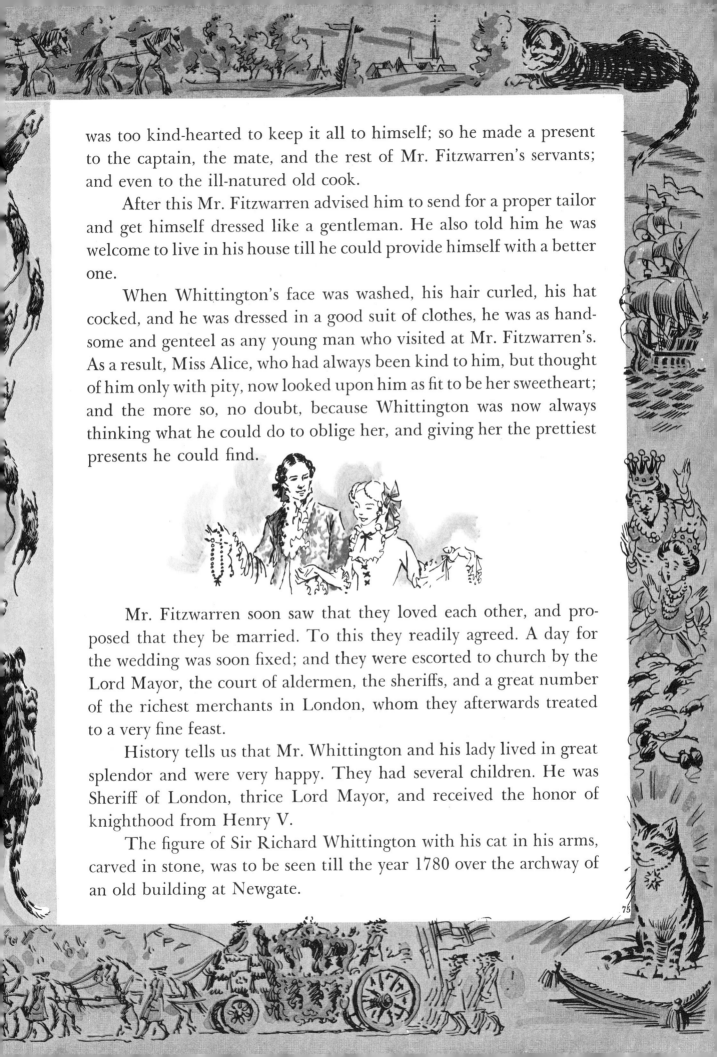

Mr. Fitzwarren soon saw that they loved each other, and proposed that they be married. To this they readily agreed. A day for the wedding was soon fixed; and they were escorted to church by the Lord Mayor, the court of aldermen, the sheriffs, and a great number of the richest merchants in London, whom they afterwards treated to a very fine feast.

History tells us that Mr. Whittington and his lady lived in great splendor and were very happy. They had several children. He was Sheriff of London, thrice Lord Mayor, and received the honor of knighthood from Henry V.

The figure of Sir Richard Whittington with his cat in his arms, carved in stone, was to be seen till the year 1780 over the archway of an old building at Newgate.

The Legend of Sleepy Hollow

ILLUSTRATED BY ARTHUR RACKHAM

O**N THE EASTERN SHORE** of the Hudson there is a small town known as Tarry Town. Not far from this village there is a little valley among high hills which is one of the quietest places in the whole world. A small brook glides through it and the occasional whistle of a quail or tapping of a woodpecker is almost the only sound heard.

This quiet glen has long been known by the name of SLEEPY HOLLOW. The inhabitants are descendants of the original Dutch settlers. A dreamy influence seems to hang over the land. Some say that the place was bewitched during the early days of the settlement by a German doctor. Others claim that an old Indian chief, the prophet or wizard of his tribe, held his powwows there before the country was discovered by Master Hendrik Hudson. The whole neighborhood abounds with local tales, haunted spots, and twilight superstitions.

The dominant spirit that haunts this enchanted region is the apparition of a figure on horseback without a head. It is said by some to be the ghost of a Hessian trooper whose head had been carried away by a cannonball in a battle of the Revolutionary War. Certain historians allege that because the body of the trooper is buried in the churchyard in Sleepy Hollow, the ghost rides forth to the scene of battle in nightly quest of his head. The speed with which he sometimes passes along the Hollow is owing to his haste to get back to the churchyard before daybreak. The specter is known at all the country firesides as the Headless Horseman of Sleepy Hollow.

Now in Sleepy Hollow there lived a prosperous farmer, Baltus Van Tassel by name, whose farm stretched to the banks of the Hudson. His house nestled under a great elm tree with broad branches. Nearby was a vast barn, every window and crevice bursting with the treasures of the farm. Sleepy porkers grunted in their pens, while little piglets ran underfoot. Snowy geese waddled near a pond where ducks paddled, while flocks of turkeys gobbled through the farmyard and guinea fowls gave their mournful call.

Old Baltus Van Tassel had one child, a daughter. Katrina Van Tassel was eighteen, a lovely girl, as round and rosy-cheeked as one of her father's peaches. Her beauty was famed throughout the countryside, and so were her father's riches.

Also in this thriving hamlet was a schoolmaster named Ichabod Crane. He was tall and lank, with long arms and legs. His feet were as big as shovels, and his hands equally large, while his head was small and flat at the top. He had huge ears, large green glassy eyes, and a long snipe nose. As he strode along a hill on a windy day, his clothes fluttering, he resembled a scarecrow from a cornfield.

The schoolhouse was a low building of one large room, rudely constructed of logs. The windows were partly glazed and partly patched with pages of old copybooks. It stood in a lonely but pleasant place at the foot of a woody hill. A brook ran close by and a great birch tree grew at one end of it.

Above the low murmur of the pupils' voices, reading their lessons, Master Crane's voice would ring out:

"You, there! You, Hendrick Van Bosch! You are not studying."

"But I am, Master Crane," Hendrick would protest.

"Come up front," the schoolmaster would command, and Hendrick had no choice but to obey.

The ever-present birch rod came down on the shoulders of the luckless Hendrick with a sharp thwack! to the amusement of the other children.

Master Crane had been hired by the village elders not only for his knowledge, which was extensive, but also for his oft-repeated "Spare the rod and spoil the child!" Heads nodded in agreement and the schoolmaster enforced his belief in this maxim daily.

But this was the manner of the time and his pupils did not hold it against him. When school was out, Ichabod was companion and playmate of the larger boys, and on holiday afternoons he would escort some of the smaller ones home—if they had pretty sisters or if their mothers were good cooks. He lived and boarded with the families of his pupils, a week at a time, in turn, going the rounds of the neighborhood with all his worldly effects tied up in a cotton handkerchief.

He was popular with the farmers and their wives, for he helped with some of the smaller jobs on a farm—making hay, mending fences, watering horses, driving cows from pasture, and cutting wood for the winter fire. He would even sit with a child on one knee, rocking a cradle with his foot for hours at a time. Needless to say the mothers approved of this and in return fed the schoolmaster generously.

To eke out his slender income from teaching, Ichabod was also the singing master of the neighborhood, and picked up many bright shillings this way. Psalms were sung then, instead of hymns, and Master Crane knew them all. He led the choir on Sundays and the weekly evening practice was popular with all the young people. An occasional song would vary the hymns at these practices. Especially did the girls like Ichabod.

"You must come to tea on Thursday, Master Crane," a good frau would say.

And on a Thursday Master Crane was at a hospitable hearth, where a silver teapot was brought out, accompanied by a dish of cakes or sweetmeats. Between services on Sunday, Ichabod entertained the girls by gathering grapes for them or sauntering with a group of them along the banks of the millpond.

One Sunday he found Katrina Van Tassel in the churchyard, and to amuse her he read the epitaphs from the tombstones, some of which were quaint indeed.

"See, Mistress Katrina," he said, "here's one poor lad. It says, 'By love he was undone.' Alas, that is true of all of us. Love will ever undo a man. It is because you maidens are so hardhearted."

Katrina dimpled at him. "But Master Crane," she said, "why are not the men braver? They are so tongue-tied. Pretty phrases do not come to their lips. I wish that the young men of Sleepy Hollow had your wit and grace of speech."

Ichabod was delighted. "Mistress Katrina!" he exclaimed. "May I dare hope you will listen to me? Ah, there is a song we are going to have at our next practice. I yearn to teach it to you."

And the town boys, most of them bashful country bumpkins,

would hang back, glowering, envying the schoolmaster's superior elegance and manner.

Ichabod was a kind of traveling newspaper, too.

"Ah, Mistress Van Brock," he would say in his most courtly style, as he paused at her front door in time for tea, "and have you heard what Mistress Van Tassel thinks of the new style in bonnets from Boston?"

And Mistress Van Brock would eagerly ask him in to relate the latest gossip as he feasted at her lavish tea table.

Master Crane was actually known to have read several books all the way through, and he knew well Cotton Mather's history of New England witchcraft. He believed wholeheartedly in this book and knew it by heart. After school, stretched out on a rich bed of clover, he would read old Mather's direful tales until the gathering dusk made the printed page a mere mist before his eyes. On his way home to the farmhouse where he was staying that week, he would imagine that all the sounds of nature were supernatural—the

moan of the whippoorwill from the hillside, the boding cry of the treetoad, the dreary hooting of the screech owl, or the sudden rustling in the thicket of birds frightened from their roost.

Many a long winter evening did the schoolmaster pass by a blazing fire when a good wife sat spinning. The Dutch fraus had marvelous tales of ghosts and goblins, haunted fields, brooks, bridges and houses. The story most often told was that of the Headless Horseman, or Galloping Hessian of the Hollow. In turn, Ichabod would delight them equally by his anecdotes of witchcraft and speculations on the heavens.

"Indeed, ma'am," he would assure the industrious spinner, "I myself have seen a comet. Some think it means the end of the world, but not I. Are we not still here?"

And again he would say: "Did you know that the world turns absolutely around? 'Tis a fact. I have read it with my own eyes in a most scholarly book. Half the time we're topsy-turvy indeed!"

"Ah, Master Crane," the Dutch wife would murmur, "how much you know, to be sure."

His courage was high by the chimney corner and the crackling wood fire, but walking back at night to the farmhouse where he was staying that week was something else. Ichabod's path was beset by fearful shapes and shadows amid the dim and ghastly glare of a snowy night! How often a rushing blast howling in the trees sounded to his fearful ears like the Galloping Hessian himself on one of his nightly rounds!

Still, Master Crane's life would have run smoothly had it not been for the lovely Katrina Van Tassel. It was not only her beauty that stirred him. After seeing the riches of her father's farm, all of which she would one day inherit, Ichabod determined this prize was for him. His mouth watered as he thought of the feasts ahead of him — pigs roasted with apples in their mouths, geese swimming in their own gravy, ducks with onion sauce, sleek sides of bacon, juicy hams, turkeys with necklaces of savory sausages.

His great green eyes roved over the fat meadowlands and his

heart yearned after the damsel who was to inherit these domains. Even the farmhouse itself was after his own heart, a spacious dwelling with high-ridged but lowly sloping roofs, built in the style handed down from the first Dutch settlers. The low projecting eaves formed a piazza along the front that could be closed in bad weather. From the piazza Ichabod entered the hall, which formed the center of the mansion. Rows of resplendent pewter ranged on a long dresser dazzled his eyes. In one corner stood a huge bag of wool ready to be spun. Ears of Indian corn and strings of dried apples and peaches hung in gay festoons along the walls, mingled with red peppers. A door left ajar gave him a peep into the best parlor where the claw-footed chairs and dark mahogany tables shone like mirrors. A corner cupboard, knowingly left open, displayed immense treasures of old silver and china.

"How may I gain her affections?" Ichabod asked himself. "She must be mine!"

But the schoolmaster had two major difficulties. One was Katrina herself, who was a heartless coquette. The other was a host of rustic admirers always at her heels. The most formidable of these was a burly, roaring, roistering blade named Abraham Van Brunt, or Brom for short. He towered over his companions, and could whip any man in hand-to-hand combat, run faster than anyone else in the countryside, and shout louder than the thunder itself. Indeed, because of his Herculean frame and great powers of limb, his nickname was Brom Bones.

He had three or four boon companions who acknowledged him as their head, and this gang scoured the country. They went to every party or fight for miles around. Often, when the clock struck midnight, there would be a pounding of hoofs on the road, and with a whoop and a halloa the wild horsemen would rush by like a troop of Don Cossacks.

A goodman and his wife would awake, startled out of their sleep.

"Ay, there goes Brom Bones and his gang," the wife would

groan, while her husband spat out a harsh word for those who shattered his sleep.

Whenever there was a madcap prank or rustic brawl, eyebrows lifted and heads wagged knowingly.

"Brom Bones, I warrant," one would say, and the others would nod agreement.

Now Brom loved Katrina and it was whispered that she did not discourage him. When he called on her, his rivals withdrew without protest. When Brom's horse, Daredevil, was hitched to the Van Tassels' paling on a Sunday night, all other suitors passed by in despair.

This did not discourage Ichabod Crane. He had a happy mixture of pliability and perseverance in his nature. He was yielding but tough. Though he bent, he never broke, and though he bowed beneath the slightest pressure, yet the moment it was gone he was again erect and carried his head as high as ever. He was wise enough not to take the field openly against Brom Bones. He made his advances to his love in a quiet and gently insinuating manner. As the singing master of the hamlet, he made frequent visits to the farmhouse.

He had no trouble with Katrina's parents. Baltus Van Tassel was an indulgent father, who loved his daughter better even than his pipe and let her have her way in everything. Mistress Van Tassel had enough to do to attend to her housekeeping and manage her poultry.

"Ducks and geese are foolish things," she often said, nodding sagely, "and must be looked after. Girls can take care of themselves."

So she bustled about the house or sat at her spinning wheel at one end of the piazza, while Baltus smoked his evening pipe at the other, and Ichabod courted Katrina by the spring under the great elm, or strolled with her in the twilight.

"You will be at the singing school tomorrow evening, Mistress Katrina, will you not?" he asked on one of these strolls.

Katrina dimpled. "Yes, I think so. Why not?"

"I am glad," Ichabod declared. "When you are not there it is like a desert and I am alone upon it. But when you are there — it is heaven itself!"

Katrina lowered her eyes shyly. "What is the new song, Master Crane? You mentioned there was to be one on Sunday, I remember."

"A simple love song, fair lady. May I sing it for you?"

Katrina nodded.

So Master Crane made progress! Brom was out of Katrina's favor and he was furious. His horse was no longer seen tied at the palings on Sunday nights. Soon a deadly feud grew between Brom and the schoolmaster of Sleepy Hollow.

Brom wanted to fight, knowing he would win easily. But Ichabod knew that too and refused to take up the challenge. Brom resorted to boorish practical jokes, aided by his gang. One night they smoked out the singing school by stopping up the chimney. Another night they set a hound to howling along with the singers. A third evening they broke into the schoolhouse and turned everything upside down. And Brom always made a point of ridiculing Ichabod in Katrina's presence.

On the last day of October, a horseman clattered up to the door of the schoolhouse on a ragged, wild, unbroken colt, which he managed with a rope by way of halter. Ichabod sat on his lofty stool, watching his pupils who were all busy studying or whispering slyly behind their hands.

"Master Crane," the messenger called, "I bring you an invitation to a merrymaking at Mynheer Van Tassel's this evening. 'Tis a quilting frolic, and you are asked to be there."

So saying, he dashed over the brook and was seen scampering up the hollow on his odd-looking steed.

All was now bustle and hubbub in the late quiet schoolroom. The scholars were hurried through their lessons. Books were flung aside without being put away on the shelves, inkstands were overturned, benches thrown down, and the whole school was turned loose an hour before the usual time.

The gallant Ichabod now spent at least an extra half hour getting himself ready.

"I must look my best," he told himself; as he peered into the bit of broken looking glass that hung in the schoolhouse. He brushed his rusty black suit with especial care and smoothed his hair.

To make a good impression on his lady love, he borrowed a horse from Hans Van Ripper, the farmer at whose house he was staying that week. Although the animal was a broken-down plow-horse that had lost one eye, he must have had fire and mettle in his day, for he was named Gunpowder. He had once been a favorite steed of his master's, for Van Ripper was a furious rider and had infused some of his own spirit into the animal. Old and broken-down as he looked, there was more of the lurking devil in Gunpowder than in any young filly in the country.

Ichabod did not look like a knight errant. He rode with short

stirrups, which brought his knees nearly up to the pommel of his saddle. His sharp elbows stuck out like a grasshopper's and he carried his whip perpendicularly in his hand like a scepter. As his horse jogged on, the motion of his arms was not unlike the flappings of wings. A small wool hat rested on the top of his nose, for so his scanty strip of forehead might be called, and the skirts of his black coat fluttered out almost to the horse's tail.

It was a fine autumn day, the afternoon of All Saints' Eve — Halloween. As Ichabod jogged slowly on his way his eye ranged with delight over the treasures of the autumn. On all sides he beheld vast stores of apples. Farther on were great fields of Indian corn, holding the promise of cakes and hasty pudding. The yellow pumpkins lying beneath them gave ample prospects of the most luxurious of pies. Soon he passed the fragrant buckwheat fields, breathing the odor of the beehive. Soft anticipation stole over his mind of dainty flapjacks, well buttered and garnished with honey or treacle by the delicate little dimpled hand of Katrina Van Tassel.

"Mine, all mine," he mused, "and soon."

He looked out over the mighty Hudson and saw the sun gradually wheeling his broad disk down into the west. It was toward evening that he arrived at the castle of Herr Van Tassel. The pride and flower of the countryside thronged the big house. The one who dominated the scene, though, was Brom Bones. He had come on his horse Daredevil which no one but himself could manage. He swaggered around, looking as if he knew something no one else knew.

The charms of the buxom Dutch maidens, all pink and white, were as nothing in Master Crane's sight as the ample charms of a genuine Dutch country tea table in the sumptuous time of autumn. There were heaped-up platters of many kinds of cakes. There was the doughty doughnut and the crisp and crumbling cruller. There were sweet cakes and short cakes, ginger cakes and honey cakes. Then there were apple pies and peach pies and pumpkin pies, besides slices of ham and smoked beef. There were preserved plums, peaches, pears, and quinces, not to mention broiled shad and roasted chickens. All this, with bowls of milk and cream, mingled higgledy-piggledy, with the motherly teapot sending up its clouds of vapor.

Ichabod Crane did justice to every dainty. His spirits rose as he ate and the slight uneasiness caused by Brom's swaggering disappeared. He rolled his large eyes and chuckled.

"One day I may be lord of all this luxury and splendor," he thought. "Ah, how quickly I will turn my back upon the old schoolhouse. I'll snap my fingers in the face of Hans Van Ripper. I'll kick any itinerant schoolmaster out of doors that dares call me comrade!"

His foot shot out and he nearly tripped old Baltus Van Tassel, who moved among his guests with a face as round and jolly as the harvest moon.

"Whoa, there, Master Crane!" he roared. "Have a care." He gave Ichabod an affectionate slap on the shoulder. "Fall to and help yourself, as indeed I see you have. Eat up. There is plenty more."

The sound of the fiddle in the corner caused the throng to stop eating. It was time for the dance!

Ichabod put down his well-cleaned plate and smoothed his hair.

89

He prided himself upon his dancing as much as on his vocal powers. Once when he was dancing he had heard an old burgher say:

"I swear, he looks like St. Vitus himself! Not a limb is idle!"

Quickly he crossed the big room and bowed before Katrina.

"Mistress Van Tassel," he said, "may I have the pleasure of your company in this dance?"

Without a glance at Brom who hovered nearby, Katrina put out her hand. Smiling graciously, she said, "You may, Master Crane. I will be glad to dance with you."

They danced and Katrina ignored Brom, who sat brooding by himself in a corner, sorely smitten with love and jealousy.

When the dance was ended, Ichabod was attracted to a knot of the sager folk who, with old Van Tassel, sat smoking at one end of the piazza, gossiping over former times. As Ichabod neared them, he saw that several of the Sleepy Hollow squires were present, talking of the wild and wonderful legends of their neighborhood.

"Aye," said one old codger, "I once saw a long funeral train in the dead of night. Not a word was said. They marched on and on."

"And what were you doing out that time of night?" another interrupted rudely. "I myself have heard, and not so late at night either, cries of mourning and wailings around the great tree where Major André was captured."

"Oh, everybody knows that," a third man broke in. "I too have heard those wails. But Raven Rock is the place you want to be on a dark night. The woman in white will surely be there. She comes, so they say, on a winter night before a storm, for she perished there in the snow and thus gives warning."

The chief part of the stories, however, turned upon the favorite specter of Sleepy Hollow, the Headless Horseman.

"He's been heard riding hard several times of late, I understand," one gaffer remarked. "Patroling the country again. I wonder why he's so restless now. They even say he tethers his horse nightly among the graves in the churchyard."

There was much shaking of heads and mutterings at this, as the men went on to detail other things seen and heard on dark nights.

" 'Tis always a favorite haunt of troubled spirits," one said. "The location is good for it."

The church stood on a knoll surrounded by locust trees and lofty elms. On one side extended a wide woody dell, along which ran a large brook among broken rocks and trunks of fallen trees. Over a deep black part of the stream not far from the church was a wooden bridge. The road that led to it and the bridge itself were thickly shaded by overhanging trees which cast a gloom about it even in the daytime. This was indeed one of the favorite haunts of the Headless Horseman and the place where he was most frequently encountered.

As Ichabod listened now to the group swapping stories, one man said:

" 'Twasn't so long ago that old Brouwer met the Horseman returning from his foray into Sleepy Hollow. Do you know what the Hessian made poor old Brouwer do? Get up behind him on that horse! And they galloped over hill and swamp until they reached the bridge. Then suddenly the Horseman turned into a skeleton, threw old Brouwer into the brook, and sprang away over the treetops with a clap of thunder. Old Brouwer was scared out of his wits. He didn't go outdoors for two weeks."

A new voice spoke up. It was Brom Bones.

"That's nothing!" he proclaimed in a deep baritone. "I was coming back one night from our neighboring village down the road, Sing Sing, and the Hessian overtook me. I could hear the hoofs pounding on the road but Daredevil was no match for that horse. He pulled up alongside and offered to race with me for a bowl of punch. He would have won it, too," Brom added ruefully, "but just as we came to the church bridge the Hessian bolted. He vanished in a flash of fire."

Then it was Ichabod's turn and he related many marvelous events that had taken place in his native state, Connecticut, and fearful sights he had seen in his nightly walks about Sleepy Hollow.

After that, the revel broke up gradually. Ichabod lingered for a tête-a-tête with the beautiful Katrina, but he found her unreceptive. She not only refused to talk to him but said:

"I shall not be at home to you any longer, Master Crane. Nor shall I continue at the singing school. You are not welcome here."

Ichabod left in a discontented mood and in the stable roused Gunpowder with several hearty cuffs and kicks. Something had gone very wrong. But what? For the life of him he could not understand Katrina's change of heart.

By the time horse and man were on the road, it was indeed the witching hour of midnight. Ichabod was not only heavy-hearted at the way his wooing had gone awry, but he had a feeling that some of the men in the group had been laughing at him. He pondered this, as well as all the stories of ghosts and goblins that had been told that evening. The night grew darker and darker. The stars seemed to sink deeper in the sky. He had never felt so lonely and dismal.

Suddenly he realized he was approaching the very scene of many of the ghost stories. In the center of the road stood an enormous tulip tree which towered like a giant above all the other trees, a kind of landmark. It was connected with the tragic story of the unfortunate British officer, André, who had been taken prisoner near there, and was universally known as Major André's Tree.

As Ichabod approached the fearful tree, he began to whistle. He thought his whistle was answered but it was merely a blast sweeping sharply through the dry branches. As he came nearer he thought he saw something white hanging in the midst of the tree. He paused and stopped whistling.

"Oh," he said to himself in relief, " 'tis only a place where lightning hit and laid bare the white wood."

Suddenly he heard a groan. His teeth chattered and his knees knocked against the saddle. Yet it was only the rubbing of one huge bough upon another as they swayed about in the breeze. He passed the tree in safety but new perils lay before him.

About two hundred yards from the tree a small brook crossed the road and ran into a marshy and thickly wooded glen known as Wiley's Swamp. A few rough logs laid side by side served for a bridge

over this stream. On that side of the road where the brook entered the wood, a group of oaks and chestnuts, matted thick with wild grapevines, threw a cavernous gloom over it. To pass this bridge was the severest trial, for it was at this identical spot that André was captured.

As Ichabod approached the stream, his heart began to thump. He summoned up all his resolution.

"Giddyap, Gunpowder," he said with a courage he did not feel. He gave his horse half a score of kicks in the ribs and attempted to dash briskly across the bridge.

But instead of starting forward, the animal ran broadside against the fence. Ichabod, whose fears increased with delay, jerked the reins on the other side. It was all in vain. His steed started, but it was only to plunge to the opposite side of the road into a thicket of brambles and alder bushes. The schoolmaster now bestowed both whip and heel upon old Gunpowder's ribs. The horse dashed forward, snuffling and snorting, but came to a stand just by the bridge with a suddenness that nearly sent his rider sprawling over his head.

Just at this moment a tramping by the side of the bridge caught the sensitive ear of Ichabod. In the dark shadow of the grove he beheld something huge, misshapen, black and towering. Ichabod's hair rose upon his head with terror.

"What shall I do?" he asked himself frantically. "It's too late to turn and fly. And how can I escape a ghost or goblin which can ride upon wings of the wind?"

The schoolmaster summoned up a show of courage. "Who — who—are y-y-you?" he demanded in a stammering voice.

There was no reply.

"Who — who — a-a-a-re — y-y-y-you?" he asked again, in a still more agitated voice.

Still there was no answer.

Once more Ichabod kicked Gunpowder's sides and, shutting his eyes, began to sing a psalm. Just then the shadowy object of alarm put itself in motion. With a scramble and a bound it stood in the middle of the road. Ichabod had opened his eyes and he saw what appeared to be a horseman of large size, mounted on a black horse of powerful frame. He kept aloof on one side of the road, jogging along on the blind side of old Gunpowder, now over his fright and waywardness.

Ichabod, who had no relish for this strange midnight companion, now quickened his steed, in hopes of leaving the other behind. The stranger, however, quickened his horse to an equal pace. Ichabod pulled up and fell into a walk, thinking to lag behind. The other did the same. Ichabod's heart began to sink within him. There was something in the moody and dogged silence of this companion that was mysterious and appalling. It was soon fearfully accounted for.

On mounting a rise in the ground the figure of his fellow traveler was brought into relief against the sky. It was gigantic in height and muffled in a cloak, but Ichabod was horror-struck to perceive that he was headless! The schoolmaster's horror was still more increased on observing that the head, which should have rested on the stranger's shoulders, was carried before him on the pommel of the saddle.

Ichabod's terror rose to desperation. He rained a shower of kicks and blows on Gunpowder, hoping by a sudden movement to give his companion the slip. But the specter started full jump with him. Away then they dashed, through thick and thin, stones flying and sparks flashing at every bound. Ichabod's flimsy garments fluttered in the air as he stretched his long lank body over his horse's head in the eagerness of his flight.

They had now reached the road which turned off to Sleepy Hollow. But Gunpowder, seemingly possessed with a demon, instead of keeping on the road made an opposite turn and plunged headlong downhill to the left.

95

Until now the panic of the steed had given his unskillful rider an apparent advantage in the chase. But just as he had got halfway through the hollow, the girths of the saddle gave way and Ichabod felt it slipping from under him. He seized it by the pommel and endeavored to hold it firm, but in vain. He had just time to save himself by clasping old Gunpowder around the neck when the saddle fell to the earth and he heard it trampled underfoot by his pursuer.

For a moment the terror of Hans Van Ripper's wrath passed across Ichabod's mind, for it was his Sunday saddle. But this was not the time for petty fears. The goblin was hard on his haunches and, unskillful rider that he was, he had all he could do to maintain

his seat. Sometimes he slipped on one side, sometimes on the other, and sometimes he jolted on the high ridge of the horse's backbone with a violence that he feared would tear him apart.

An opening in the trees now cheered him with the hope that the church bridge was at hand. He saw the walls of the church dimly glaring under the trees beyond. He recollected the place where Brom Bones's ghostly competitor had disappeared.

"If I can but reach that bridge," thought Ichabod, "I am safe."

Just then he heard the black steed panting and blowing close behind him. He even fancied that he felt his hot breath. Another convulsive kick in the ribs and old Gunpowder sprang upon the bridge. He thundered over the resounding planks and gained the opposite side. Now Ichabod cast a look behind to see if his pursuer should vanish, according to rule, in a flash of fire and brimstone.

Just then he saw the goblin rising in his stirrups and in the very act of hurling his head at him! Ichabod tried to dodge the horrible missile, but too late. It struck his head with a tremendous crack and he was tumbled headlong into the dust. Gunpowder, the black steed, and the goblin rider passed by like a whirlwind.

The next morning Gunpowder was found without his saddle, and with the bridle under his feet, soberly cropping the grass at his master's gate. Ichabod did not make his appearance at breakfast. Dinner hour came but no Ichabod. The boys assembled at the schoolhouse and strolled idly about the banks of the brook. Still there was no sign of the schoolmaster.

"Where is Master Crane?" someone asked.

Knowing looks were exchanged and at least one boy giggled, but nothing more was said.

Hans Van Ripper now began to feel some uneasiness about the fate of poor Ichabod and of his saddle. An inquiry was set on foot and after diligent investigation some men came upon his traces. In one part of the road leading to the church was found the saddle trampled in the dirt. The tracks of horses' hoofs were traced to the

97

bridge beyond which, where the water ran deep and black, was found the hat of the unfortunate Ichabod. Close beside it lay a shattered pumpkin.

The brook was searched but the body of the schoolmaster was not found. Hans Van Ripper, as executor of Ichabod's estate, examined the bundle which contained all the pedant's worldly effects. They consisted of two shirts and a half, two stocks for the neck, a pair or two of worsted stockings, an old pair of corduroy small clothes, a rusty razor, a book of psalm tunes, and a broken pitchpipe.

The mysterious event caused much speculation at the church on the following Sunday.

"Do you suppose he rode with the Hessian as did old Brouwer?" one man asked a knot of gazers and gossips collected in the churchyard.

"I'll warrant he raced with the goblin as did Brom Bones," another said to a group at the bridge.

"That pumpkin," mused a third aloud to those who had gathered at the spot where the hat and the pumpkin had been found. "It bears a remarkable resemblance to a human head."

But they all shook their own heads.

"Nay," said the old gaffer who had told most of the stories at the Van Tassels' dance, "the schoolmaster was carried off by the Galloping Hessian. I am sure of it."

And that was the end of the matter, for as Ichabod was a bachelor and not in debt, nobody troubled his head any more about him. The school was removed to a different quarter of the hollow and another schoolmaster reigned in his stead.

Several years passed. Then an old farmer who had been down to New York on a visit brought home the news that Ichabod Crane was still alive. He gladly told the story to anyone who would listen.

"He left hereabouts," he related, "because he was afraid of the goblin and what Hans Van Ripper would do to him for losing his saddle, and also because Mistress Van Tassel, the heiress, dismissed him that night, and he was mortified. He went a-purpose to a distant part of the country.

"Yes, he went on keeping school," the farmer continued, "but he studied law, too, and was admitted to the bar. I heard he then turned politician, electioneered, wrote for the newspapers, and finally was made a justice of the Ten Pound Court."

And that was the story that Sleepy Hollow buzzed with for days. But at least one person looked knowing indeed when he heard it — Brom Bones. Shortly after his rival's disappearance, Brom had led the blooming Katrina in triumph to the altar. He, not Ichabod, achieved the broad acres of the Van Tassel farm, the rich treasures of its bursting barns and fields, and the beautiful daughter of old Baltus. And ever after, when the story of Ichabod was told, Brom looked wise and always burst into a hearty laugh at the mention of the pumpkin. This led some to suspect that he knew more about the matter than he chose to tell.

The old country wives, however, are the best judges of these matters.

"It was the Hessian," one said to another firmly. "He carried poor Master Crane away with him. I'm certain of it."

Her friend nodded agreement. "Yes, it was the Headless Horseman. I am sure of it, too. He made off with the schoolmaster and we will never see him again."

Whether Ichabod was spirited away by supernatural means, or whether the farmer's account was true, the tale of the Headless Horseman and the schoolmaster is a favorite story often told about the neighborhood around the winter evening fire.

Rapunzel

ILLUSTRATED BY LOWELL HESS

O NCE UPON A TIME THERE WERE a man and a woman who had long in vain wished for a child. At last the woman hoped that God was about to grant her desire.

This couple had a little window at the back of their house from which a splendid garden could be seen. It was full of the most beautiful flowers and herbs. It was, however, surrounded by a high wall, and no one dared to go into it because it belonged to a Witch named Dame Gothel who had great power and was dreaded by all the world.

One day, the woman was standing by this window and looking down into the garden, when she saw a bed which was planted with the most beautiful rampion (rapunzel). It looked so fresh and green that she longed for it, and had the greatest desire to eat some.

This desire increased every day, and as she knew that she could not get any of it, she quite pined away, and looked pale and miserable.

Then her husband was alarmed, and asked, "What ails you, dear wife?"

"Ah," she replied, "if I can't get to eat some of the rampion which is in the garden behind our house, I shall die."

The man, who loved her, thought, "Sooner than let her die, I'll bring her some of the rampion myself, let it cost me what it will!"

So, in the twilight of evening, he clambered over the wall into the garden of the Witch, hastily clutched a handful of rampion, and took it to his wife. She at once made herself a salad of it, and ate it with much relish.

However, she liked it so much—so very much—that the next day she longed for it three times as much as before. If he was to have any rest, her husband must once more descend into the garden. In the gloom of evening, therefore, he let himself down again. But when he had clambered down the wall he was terribly afraid, for he saw the Witch standing before him.

"How dare you," said she with an angry look, "descend into my garden and steal my rampion like a thief? You shall suffer for it!"

"Ah," answered he, "let mercy take the place of justice! I had to do it. My wife saw your rampion from the window, and felt such a longing for it that she would have died if she had not got some to eat."

At this the Witch let her anger be softened, and said to him, "If the case be as you say, I will allow you to take away with you as much rampion as you wish. I make only one condition: you must give me the child which your wife will bring into the world. It shall be well treated, and I will care for it like a mother."

In his terror the man consented to everything. And when the woman at last had a little daughter, the Witch appeared at once, gave the child the name of Rapunzel, and took it away with her.

Rapunzel grew into the most beautiful child under the sun. When she was twelve years old, the Witch shut her into a tower, which lay in a forest, and had neither stairs nor door. But at the very top there was a little window. When the Witch wanted to go in, she placed herself beneath this window and cried:

> *"Rapunzel, Rapunzel,*
> *Let down thy hair."*

Rapunzel had magnificent long hair, fine as spun gold, and when she heard the voice of the Witch, she unfastened her braided tresses and wound them around one of the hooks of the window. Then she let the hair fall twenty stories down, and the Witch climbed up by it.

After a year or two, it came to pass that the King's son rode through the forest and went by the tower. Suddenly he heard a song. It was so charming that he stood still and listened. The voice belonged to Rapunzel, who in her solitude passed her time in letting her sweet voice resound.

The King's son wanted to climb up to her, and he looked for the door of the tower, but there was none to be found. He rode home, but the singing had so deeply touched his heart that every day he went out into the forest and listened to it.

Once when he was thus standing behind a tree, he saw that a Witch came there, and he heard how she cried:

> *"Rapunzel, Rapunzel,*
> *Let down thy hair."*

Then Rapunzel let down the braids of her hair, and the Witch climbed up to her. "If that is the ladder by which one mounts, I will for once try my fortune," said the King's son.

The next day when it began to grow dark, he went to the tower and cried: *"Rapunzel, Rapunzel,*
Let down thy hair."

Immediately the hair fell down, and the King's son climbed up.

At first Rapunzel was terribly frightened, for she had never before seen a man. But the King's son began to talk to her quite like a

friend, and told her that his heart had been so stirred that it had let him have no rest, so he had been forced to see her.

Then Rapunzel lost her fear, and when he asked her if she would take him for her husband, and she saw that he was young and handsome, she thought, "He will love me more than old Dame Gothel does." So she said yes, and laid her hand in his.

She said also, "I will willingly go away with you, but I do not know how to get down. Bring with you a skein of silk every time that you come, and I will weave a ladder with it. When that is ready I will descend, and you can take me on your horse."

They agreed that until that time, the King's son should come to her every evening, for the old woman came by day. The Witch knew nothing of this until one day when Rapunzel said to her, "Tell me, Dame Gothel, how is it that you are so much heavier for me to draw up than the King's son? He is with me in a moment."

"Ah! You wicked child!" cried the Witch. "What do I hear you say! I thought I had separated you from all the world, and yet you have deceived me!"

In her anger she clutched Rapunzel's beautiful tresses, wrapped them twice around her left hand, seized a pair of scissors with the right, and *snip, snap,* the lovely braids were cut off and lay on the ground. Nor was that all. The Witch was so pitiless that she took poor Rapunzel into a desert, where she had to live in great grief and misery.

On the same day, however, that she cast out Rapunzel, the Witch, in the evening, fastened the braids of hair which she had cut off, to the hook of the window; and when the King's son came and cried:

> *"Rapunzel, Rapunzel,*
> *Let down thy hair."*

she let the hair down.

The King's son ascended. He did not find his dearest Rapunzel above, but only the Witch, who gazed at him with wicked and venomous looks.

"Aha!" she cried mockingly. "You would fetch your dearest!

But the beautiful bird no longer sits singing in the nest. The cat has got it, and will scratch out your eyes as well. Rapunzel is lost to you! You will never see her again!"

The King's son was beside himself with grief and in his despair he leaped down from the tower. He escaped with his life, but the

thorns into which he fell pierced his eyes. Then he wandered quite blind about the forest, ate nothing but roots and berries, and did nothing but lament and weep over the loss of his beloved.

Thus he roamed about in misery for some years. At last he came to the desert where Rapunzel lived in wretchedness. He heard a voice, and it seemed so familiar to him that he went toward it. When he approached, Rapunzel knew him, and fell on his neck and wept. Two of her tears wetted his eyes and they grew clear again, and he could see with them as before.

Then the King's son led Rapunzel to his kingdom where he was joyfully received, and they lived for a long time, happy and contented.

Ali Baba
and the Forty Thieves

ILLUSTRATED BY PETER MARKS

IN A TOWN IN PERSIA there dwelt two brothers, one named Cassim, the other Ali Baba. Cassim was married to a rich wife and lived in plenty, while Ali Baba had to maintain his wife and children by cutting wood in a neighboring forest and selling it in the town. One day, when Ali Baba was in the forest, he saw a troop of men on horseback coming toward him in a cloud of dust. He was afraid they were robbers and climbed into a tree for safety. When they came up to him and dismounted, he counted forty of them. They unbridled their horses and tied them to trees.

The finest man among them, whom Ali Baba took to be their captain, went a little way among some bushes and said, "Open, Sesame!" so plainly that Ali Baba heard him. A door opened in the rocks and, having made the troop go in, the captain followed them and the door shut again of itself.

They stayed sometime inside and Ali Baba, fearing they might come out and catch him, was forced to sit patiently in the tree. At last the door opened again and the forty thieves came out. As the captain went in last he came out first, and made the others all pass by him; he then closed the door, saying, "Shut, Sesame!" Every man bridled his horse and mounted, the captain put himself at their head, and they returned as they had come.

Then Ali Baba climbed down and went to the door concealed among the bushes and said, "Open, Sesame!" and it flew open. Ali Baba, who expected a dull, dismal place, was greatly surprised to find it large and well lighted, and hollowed by the hand of man in the form of a vault, which received the light from an opening in the ceiling. He saw rich bales of merchandise—silk stuffs, brocades, all piled together, gold and silver in heaps, and money in leather purses. He went in and the door shut behind him. He did not look at the silver but brought out as many bags of gold as he thought his donkeys, which were browsing outside, could carry, loaded them with the bags, and hid it all with fagots. Then using the words, "Shut, Sesame!" he closed the door and went home.

Arriving there, he drove his donkeys into the yard, shut the gates, carried the moneybags to his wife, and emptied them out before her. He bade her keep the secret and said he would bury the gold.

"Let me first measure it," said his wife. "I will borrow a measure from someone while you dig the hole."

So she ran to the wife of Cassim and borrowed a measure. Cassim's wife was curious to find out what sort of grain Ali Baba's wife wished to measure and artfully put some suet at the bottom of the measure. Ali Baba's wife went home and set the measure on the heap of gold and filled it and emptied it often, to her great content. She then returned the measure, without noticing that a piece of gold was sticking to it.

Cassim's wife grew very curious and said to Cassim when he came home, "Cassim, your brother is richer than you. He does not count his money, he measures it."

He begged her to explain this riddle, which she did by showing him the piece of money and telling him where she had found it. Then Cassim grew so envious that he could not sleep and went to his brother in the morning before sunrise.

"Ali Baba," he said, showing him the gold piece, "you pretend to be poor and yet you measure gold."

By this Ali Baba perceived that through his wife's folly Cassim and his wife knew his secret, so he confessed all and offered Cassim a share.

"That I expect," said Cassim, "but I must know where to find the treasure, otherwise I will discover all and you will lose all."

Ali Baba, more out of kindness than fear, told him of the cave and the very words to use. Cassim left Ali Baba, meaning to be beforehand with him and get the treasure for himself. He rose early next morning and set out with ten mules loaded with great chests. He soon found the place and the door in the rock. He said, "Open, Sesame!" and the door opened and shut behind him.

He could have feasted his eyes all day on the treasure, but he now hastened to gather together as much of it as possible; but when he was ready to go he could not remember what to say. Instead of "Sesame," he said, "Open, Barley!" and the door remained fast. He named several other sorts of grain, all but the right one, and still the door stuck fast. He was so frightened at the danger he was in that he had as much forgotten the word as if he had never heard it.

About noon the robbers returned to their cave and saw Cassim's mules roving about with great chests on their backs. This gave them the alarm. They drew their sabers, and went to the door, which opened upon their captain's saying, "Open, Sesame!" Cassim, who had heard the trampling of their horses' hoofs, resolved to sell his life dearly, so when the door opened he leaped out and threw the captain down. In vain, however, for the robbers with their sabers soon killed him. On entering the cave they saw all the bags laid ready, and could not imagine how anyone had got in without knowing their secret. They put Cassim's body into a sack and went away in search of more treasure.

As night drew on Cassim's wife grew very uneasy, ran to her brother-in-law, and told him where her husband had gone. Ali Baba did his best to comfort her and set out for the forest in search of Cassim. The first thing he saw on entering the cave was the sack containing his dead brother's body. Full of horror, he put the body on one of his donkeys and bags of gold on the other two and, covering all with fagots, returned home. He drove the two donkeys laden with gold into his own yard and led the other to Cassim's house. The door was opened by the slave Morgiana, whom he knew to be both brave and cunning.

Unloading the donkey, he said to her, "This is the body of your master, who has been murdered, but whom we must bury as though he had died in his bed. I will speak with you again, but now tell your mistress I have come."

The wife of Cassim, on learning the fate of her husband, broke out into cries and tears. Ali Baba offered to take her to live with him and his wife if she would promise to keep his counsel and leave everything to Morgiana; whereupon she agreed, and dried her eyes.

Morgiana, meanwhile, sought an apothecary and asked him for some lozenges. "My poor master," she said, "can neither eat nor speak and no one knows what ails him." She carried home the lozenges and returned next day weeping and asked for an essence given only to those just about to die. Thus, in the evening, no one was

surprised to hear the shrieks and cries of Cassim's wife and Morgiana, telling everyone that Cassim was dead.

The next day Morgiana went to an old cobbler near the gates of the town, put a piece of gold in his hand, and, after blindfolding him, bade him follow her with his needle and thread. She led him to the room where the body lay, took off the blindfold and bade the cobbler sew up the sack, after which she covered his eyes again and led him home.

Then Cassim was buried, and Morgiana, his slave, followed him to the grave, weeping and tearing her hair, while Cassim's wife stayed at home uttering lamentable cries. Next day she went to live with Ali Baba, who gave Cassim's shop to his eldest son.

The forty thieves, on their return to the cave, were much astonished to find Cassim's body gone as well as some of their money bags.

"We are certainly discovered," said the captain, "and shall be undone if we cannot find out who it is that knows our secret. Two men must have known it; we have killed one, we must now find the other. To this end one of you who is bold and artful must go into the city, dressed as a traveler, and discover whom we have killed and whether men talk of the strange manner of his death. If the messenger fails he must lose his life, lest we be betrayed."

One of the thieves started up and offered to do this and, after the rest had highly commended him for his bravery, he disguised himself and entered the town at daybreak, just as the cobbler was opening his stall. The thief bade him good day, saying, "Honest man, how can you possibly see to stitch at your age?"

"Old as I am," replied the cobbler, "I have good eyes, and you will believe me when I tell you that I sewed a dead body into a sack in a place where I had less light than I have now."

The robber was overjoyed at his good fortune and, giving the cobbler a piece of gold, desired to be shown the house where he had stitched up the sack. At first the old cobbler refused, saying that he had been blindfolded. But when the robber gave him another piece of gold, he began to think he might remember the street turnings if he were blindfolded as before. So this was done. The robber partly led him and was partly guided by him right in front of Cassim's house, the door of which the robber marked with a piece of chalk.

Then, well pleased, the robber bade farewell to the old cobbler and returned to the forest. By and by Morgiana, going out, saw the mark the robber had made, quickly guessed that some mischief was brewing and, fetching a piece of white chalk, marked two or three doors on each side, without saying anything to her master or mistress.

The thief, meanwhile, told his comrades of his discovery. The captain thanked him and bade him show him the house he had marked. But when they came to it they saw that five or six of the houses were chalked in the same manner. The guide was so confounded that he did not know what to say, and when they returned to the cave he was at once beheaded for having failed. Another robber

was dispatched and, having won over the old cobbler, marked Cassim's house in red chalk; but Morgiana being again too clever for the robbers, the second messenger was put to death also.

The captain now resolved to go himself but, wiser than the others, he did not mark the house but looked at it so closely he could not fail to remember it. He returned and ordered his men to go into the neighboring villages and buy ninteen mules and thirty-eight leather jars, all empty except one which was to be filled with oil. The captain put one of his men, fully armed, into each empty jar, rubbing the outsides with oil from the full vessel. Then the nineteen mules were loaded with thirty-seven robbers in jars and the jar of oil and, led by the captain, reached the town by dusk.

The captain stopped his mules in front of Ali Baba's house and said to Ali Baba, who was sitting outside enjoying the coolness, "I have brought some oil from a distance to sell at tomorrow's market, but is now so late that I do not know where to pass the night. Will you do me the favor to take me in?"

Though Ali Baba had seen the captain of the robbers in the forest, he did not recognize him in the disguise of an oil merchant. He bade him welcome, opened his gates for the mules to enter, and went to Morgiana to bid her prepare a bed and supper for his guest. He brought the stranger into his hall, and after they had supped went again to speak to Morgiana in the kitchen, while the captain went into the yard under pretense of seeing after his mules but really to tell his men what to do.

Beginning at the first jar and ending at the last, he said to each man, "As soon as I throw some stones from the bedroom upstairs, cut the jars open with your knives and come out, and I will be with you in a trice."

He returned to the house and Morgiana led him to his chamber. She then told Abdullah, her fellow slave, to start making the next day's broth for her master, who had gone to bed. Meanwhile her lamp went out and she had no more oil in the house.

"Do not be uneasy," said Abdullah. "Go into the yard and take some out of one of those jars."

Morgiana thanked him for his advice, took the oil pot, and went into the yard. When she came to the first jar the robber inside said softly, "Is it time?"

Any other slave but Morgiana, on finding a man in the jar instead of the oil she wanted, would have screamed and made a noise. But she, knowing the danger her master was in, bethought herself of a plan and answered quietly, "Not yet, but presently."

She went to all the jars, giving the same answer, till she came to the jar of oil. She now saw that her master, thinking to entertain an oil merchant, had let thirty-eight robbers into his house. She filled her oil pot, went back to the kitchen and, having lit her lamp, went again to the oil jar and filled a large kettle full of oil. When it boiled she went out again and poured enough oil into every jar to stifle and kill the robber inside. When this brave deed was done she went back to the kitchen, put out the fire and the lamp, and waited to see what would happen.

In a quarter of an hour the captain of the robbers awoke, got up and opened the window. As all seemed quiet he threw down some little pebbles which hit the jars. He listened and as none of his men seemed to stir, he grew uneasy and went down into the yard. On going to the first jar and saying "Are you asleep?" he smelled the hot boiled oil and knew at once that his plot to murder Ali Baba and his household had been discovered. He found all the members of his band dead and, missing the oil out of the last jar, became aware of the manner of their death. He then forced the lock of a door leading into a garden and, climbing over several walls, made his escape. Morgiana heard and saw all this and, rejoicing at her success, went to bed and fell asleep.

At daybreak Ali Baba arose and, seeing the oil jars there still, asked why the merchant had not gone with his mules. Morgiana bade him look in the first jar and see if there was any oil. Seeing a man there instead, he started back in terror.

"Have no fear," said Morgiana. "The man cannot harm you; he is dead."

Ali Baba, when he had recovered somewhat from his astonishment, asked what had become of the merchant.

"Merchant!" said Morgiana. "He is no more a merchant than

I am!" And she told him the whole story, assuring him that it was a plot of the robbers of the forest, and that the white and red chalk marks had something to do with it. Ali Baba at once gave Morgiana her freedom, saying that he owed her his life. They then buried the bodies in Ali Baba's garden, while the mules were sold in the market by his slaves.

The captain returned to his lonely cave, which seemed frightful to him without his lost companions, and firmly resolved to avenge them by killing Ali Baba. He dressed himself carefully and went into the town, where he took lodgings at an inn. In the course of a great many journeys to the forest he carried away many rich stuffs and much fine linen, and set up a shop opposite that of Ali Baba's son. He called himself Cogia Hassan, and as he was both civil and well dressed he soon made friends with Ali Baba's son and through him with Ali Baba, whom he was continually asking to sup with him.

Ali Baba, wishing to return his kindness, invited him into his house and received him smiling, thanking him for his kindness to his son. When the merchant was about to take his leave Ali Baba stopped him, saying, "Where are you going, sir, in such haste? Will you not stay and sup with me?"

The merchant refused, saying that he had a reason and, on Ali Baba's asking him what that was, he replied, "It is, sir, that I can eat no food that has any salt in it."

"If that is all," said Ali Baba, "let me assure you that there shall be no salt in either the meat or the bread that we eat tonight."

He went to give this order to Morgiana, who was much surprised. "Who is this man," she asked, "who eats no salt with his meat?"

"He is an honest man, Morgiana," returned Ali Baba, "therefore do as I bid you."

But she could not withstand a desire to see this strange man, so she helped Abdullah carry up the dishes and saw in a moment that Cogia Hassan was the robber captain and that he carried a dagger under his garment. "I am not surprised," she said to herself, "that this wicked man who intends to kill my master will eat no salt with him, but I will hinder his plans."

She sent up the supper by Abdullah, while she made ready for one of the boldest acts that could be thought of. When dessert had been served, Cogia Hassan was left alone with Ali Baba and his son, whom he thought to make drunk and then murder them.

Morgiana, meanwhile, put on a headdress like a dancing-girl's and clasped a girdle round her waist, from which hung a dagger with a silver hilt. Then she said to Abdullah, "Take your tabor, and let us go and entertain our master and his guest."

Abdullah took his tabor and played before Morgiana until they came to the door, where Abdullah stopped playing and Morgiana made a low curtsy.

"Come in, Morgiana," said Ali Baba, "and let Cogia Hassan see what you can do." Then, turning to his guest, he said, "She is my housekeeper."

Cogia Hassan was by no means pleased, for he feared that his chance of killing Ali Baba was gone for the present, but he pretended great eagerness to see Morgiana. So Abdullah began to play and Morgiana danced. After she had performed several dances she drew her dagger and made passes with it, sometimes pointing it at her own breast, sometimes at her master's, as if it were part of the dance. Suddenly, out of breath, she snatched the tabor from Abdullah with her left hand and, holding the dagger in her right, held out the tabor to her master. Ali Baba and his son put a piece of gold into it and Cogia Hassan, seeing that she was coming to him, pulled out his purse to make her a present. But while he was putting his hand into it Morgiana plunged the dagger into his heart.

"Unworthy girl!" cried Ali Baba and his son. "What have you done to ruin us?"

"It was to preserve you, master, not to ruin you," answered Morgiana. "See here," opening the false merchant's garment and showing the dagger, "see what an enemy you have entertained! Remember, he would eat no salt with you; what more would you have? Look at him! He is the false oil merchant and the captain of the forty thieves."

Ali Baba was so grateful to Morgiana for thus saving his life that he offered her in marriage to his son, who readily consented; and a few days after, the wedding was celebrated with great splendor.

At the end of a year Ali Baba, hearing nothing of the two remaining robbers, judged they were dead, and set out to the cave. The door opened on his saying, "Open, Sesame!" He went in and saw that nobody had been there since the captain left it. He brought away as much gold as he could carry and returned to town. He told his son the secret of the cave, which his son handed down in his turn, so the children and grandchildren of Ali Baba were rich to the end of their lives.

The Magic Fishbone

Illustrated by Sheila Greenwald

ONCE UPON A TIME THERE WAS A KING, and he had a queen; and he was the manliest of his sex, and she was the loveliest of hers. The king was, in his private profession, in the service of the government.

They had nineteen children, and were always having more. Seventeen of these children took care of the baby; and Alicia, the eldest, took care of them all. Their ages varied from seven years to seven months.

One day the king was going to the office, when he stopped at the fishmonger's to buy a pound and a half of salmon not too near the tail, which the queen (who was a careful housekeeper) had requested him to send home. Mr. Pickles, the fishmonger, said, "Certainly, sir; is there any other article? Good morning."

The king went on towards the office in a melancholy mood; for quarter-day was such a long way off, and several of the dear children were growing out of their clothes. He had not proceeded far, when Mr. Pickles's errand-boy came running after him, and said, "Sir, you didn't notice the old lady in our shop."

"What old lady?" inquired the king. "I saw none."

Now, the king had not seen any old lady because this old lady had been invisible to him, though visible to Mr. Pickles's boy.

Just then the old lady came trotting up. She was dressed in shot-silk of the richest quality, smelling of dried lavender.

"King Watkins the First, I believe?" said the old lady.

"Watkins," replied the king, "is my name."

"The papa, if I am not mistaken, of the beautiful Princess Alicia?" said the old lady.

"And of eighteen other darlings," replied the king.

"Listen. You are going to the office," said the old lady.

It instantly flashed upon the king that she must be a fairy, or how could she know that?

"You are right," said the old lady, answering his thoughts. "I am the good Fairy Grandmarina. Attend! When you return home to dinner, politely invite the Princess Alicia to have some of the salmon you bought just now."

"It may disagree with her," said the king.

The old lady became so very angry at this absurd idea that the king was quite alarmed, and humbly begged her pardon.

"We hear a great deal too much about this thing disagreeing and that thing disagreeing," said the old lady, with the greatest contempt it was possible to express. "Don't be greedy. I think you want it all yourself."

The king hung his head under this reproof, and said he wouldn't talk about things disagreeing any more.

"Be good, then," said the Fairy Grandmarina, "and don't! When the beautiful Princess Alicia consents to partake of the salmon—as I think she will—you will find she will leave a fishbone on her plate. Tell her to dry it, and to rub it, and to polish it till it shines like mother-of-pearl, and to take care of it as a present from me."

"Is that all?" asked the king.

"Don't be impatient, sir," returned the Fairy Grandmarina,

scolding him severely. "Don't catch people short before they have done speaking. Just the way with you grown-up persons."

The king again hung his head and said he wouldn't do so any more.

"Be good, then," said the Fairy Grandmarina, "and don't! Tell the Princess Alicia, with my love, that the fishbone is a magic present which can only be used once; but that it will bring her, that once, whatever she wishes for, PROVIDED SHE WISHES FOR IT AT THE RIGHT TIME. That is the message. Take care of it."

The king was beginning, "Might I ask the reason?" when the fairy became absolutely furious.

"*Will* you be good, sir?" she exclaimed, stamping her foot on the ground. "The reason for this, and the reason for that, indeed! You are always wanting the reason. No reason. There! Hoity toity me! I am sick of your grown-up reasons."

The king was extremely frightened by the old lady's flying into such a passion, and he said he was very sorry to have offended her, and he wouldn't ask for reasons any more.

"Be good, then," said the old lady, "and don't!"

With those words, Grandmarina vanished, and the king went on and on and on till he came to the office. There he wrote and wrote and wrote, till it was time to go home again. Then he politely invited the Princess Alicia, as the fairy had directed him, to partake of the salmon. And when she had enjoyed it very much, he saw the fishbone on her plate, as the fairy had told him he would, and he delivered the Fairy's message. The Princess Alicia took care to dry the bone, and to rub it, and to polish it till it shone like mother-of-pearl.

When the queen was going to get up in the morning, she said, "Oh, dear me, dear me; my head, my head!" and then she fainted.

The Princess Alicia, who happened to be looking in at the chamber door, asking about breakfast, was very much alarmed when she saw her royal mamma in this state, and she rang the bell for Peggy, which was the name of the lord chamberlain. But remembering where the smelling-bottle was, she climbed on a chair and got it; and after that she climbed on another chair to the bedside, and held the smelling-bottle to the queen's nose; and after that she jumped down and got some water; and after that she jumped up again and wetted the queen's forehead; and, in short, when the lord chamberlain came in, that dear old woman said to the little princess, "What a treasure you are! I couldn't have done it better myself!"

But that was not the worst of the good queen's illness. Oh, no! She was very ill indeed, for a long time.

The Princess Alicia kept the seventeen young princes and princesses quiet, and dressed and undressed and danced the baby, and made the kettle boil, and heated the soup, and swept the hearth, and poured out the medicine, and nursed the queen, and did all that ever she could, and was as busy, busy, busy, as busy as could be.

There were not many servants at that palace, for three reasons: because the king was short of money, because a rise in his office never seemed to come, and because quarter-day was so far off that it looked almost as far off and as little as one of the stars.

But on the morning when the queen fainted away, where was the magic fishbone? Why, there it was in the Princess Alicia's pocket! She had almost taken it out to bring the queen to life again, when she put it back, and looked for the smelling-bottle.

After the queen had come out of her swoon that morning and was dozing, the Princess Alicia hurried upstairs to tell a most particular confidential friend of hers, who was a duchess. People did suppose her to be a doll; but she was really a duchess, though nobody knew it except the princess.

This most particular secret was the secret about the magic fishbone, the history of which was well-known to the duchess, because the princess told her everything. The princess kneeled down by the bed on which the duchess was lying, full-dressed and wide-awake, and whispered the secret to her. The duchess smiled and nodded. People might have supposed that she never smiled and nodded; but she often did, though nobody knew it except the princess.

Then the Princess Alicia hurried downstairs again to keep watch in the queen's room. She often kept watch by herself in the queen's room; but every evening, while the illness lasted, she sat there watching with the king. And every evening the king sat looking at her with a cross look, wondering why she never brought out the magic fishbone.

As often as she noticed this, the Princess Alicia ran upstairs, whispered the secret to the duchess over again, and said to the duchess besides, "They think we children never have a reason or a meaning!" And the duchess, though the most fashionable duchess that ever was heard of, winked her eye.

"Alicia," said the king, one evening, when she wished him good night.

"Yes, Papa."

"What has become of the magic fishbone?"

"In my pocket, Papa."

"I thought you had lost it!"

"Oh, no, Papa!"

"Or forgotten it?"

"No, indeed, Papa."

Another time the dreadful little snapping pug dog next door made a rush at one of the young princes as he stood on the steps coming home from school, and terrified him out of his wits; and he put his hand through a pane of glass and bled, bled, bled. When the seventeen other young princes and princesses saw him bleed,

bleed, bleed, they were terrified out of their wits too, and screamed themselves black in their seventeen faces all at once.

But the Princess Alicia put her hands over all their seventeen mouths, one after another, and persuaded them to be quiet because of the sick queen. And then she put the wounded prince's hand in a basin of fresh cold water, while they stared with their twice-seventeen-are-thirty-four, put-down-four-and-carry-three, eyes, and then she looked in the hand for bits of glass, and there were fortunately no bits of glass there. And then she said to two chubby-legged princes, who were sturdy though small, "Bring me the royal rag-bag: I must snip and stitch and cut and contrive."

So the two young princes tugged at the royal rag-bag and lugged it in; and the Princess Alicia sat down on the floor, with a large pair of scissors and a needle and thread, and snipped and stitched and cut and contrived, and made a bandage, and put it on, and it fitted beautifully. And when it was all done, she saw the king, her papa, looking on by the door.

"Alicia."

"Yes, Papa."

"What have you been doing?"

"Snipping, stitching, cutting, and contriving, Papa."

"Where is the magic fishbone?"

"In my pocket, Papa."

"I thought you had lost it."

"Oh, no, Papa!"

"Or forgotten it?"

"No, indeed, Papa."

After that, she ran upstairs to the duchess, and told her what had passed, and told her the secret over again; and the duchess shook her flaxen curls and laughed with her rosy lips.

Well! and so another time the baby fell under the grate. The seventeen young princes and princesses were used to it, for they were almost always falling under the grate or down the stairs; but the baby was not used to it, and it gave him a swelled face and a black eye.

129

The way the poor little darling came to tumble was, that he was out of the Princess Alicia's lap just as she was sitting, in a great coarse apron that quite smothered her, in front of the kitchen fire, beginning to peel the turnips for the broth for dinner; and the way she came to be doing that was, that the king's cook had run away that morning with her own true love, who was a tipsy soldier.

Then the seventeen young princes and princesses, who cried at everything that happened, cried and roared. But the Princess Alicia (who couldn't help crying a little herself) quietly called to them to be still, so as not to disturb the queen upstairs, who was fast getting well, and said, "Hold your tongues, you wicked little monkeys, every one of you, while I examine Baby!"

Then she examined Baby and found that he hadn't broken anything; and she held cold iron to his poor dear eye, and smoothed his poor dear face, and he presently fell asleep in her arms. Then she said to the seventeen princes and princesses, "I am afraid to let him down yet, lest he should wake and feel pain; be good, and you shall all be cooks."

They jumped for joy when they heard that, and began making themselves cooks' caps out of old newspapers. So to one she gave the salt-box, and to one she gave the barley, and to one she gave the herbs, and to one she gave the turnips, and to one she gave the carrots, and to one she gave the onions, and to one she gave the spice-box, till they were all cooks, and all running about at work, she sitting in the middle, smothered in the great coarse apron, nursing Baby.

By and by the broth was done; and the baby woke up, smiling

like an angel, and was trusted to the sedatest princes to hold, while the other princes and princesses were squeezed into a far-off corner, for fear they should get splashed and scalded, while the Princess Alicia turned out the saucepanful of broth. When the broth came tumbling out, steaming beautifully, and smelling like a nosegay good to eat, they clapped their hands. That made the baby clap his hands; and that, and his looking as if he had a comic toothache, made all the princes and princesses laugh. So the Princess Alicia said, "Laugh and be good; and after dinner we will make him a nest on the floor in a corner, and he shall sit in his nest and see a dance of eighteen cooks."

That delighted the young princes and princesses, and they ate up all the broth, and washed up all the plates and dishes, and cleared away, and pushed the table into a corner; and then they in their cooks' caps, and the Princess Alicia in the smothering coarse apron that belonged to the cook, danced a dance of eighteen cooks before the angelic baby, who forgot his swelled face and black eye and crowed with joy.

And then, once more, the Princess Alicia saw King Watkins the First, her father, standing in the doorway looking on. He said, "What have you been doing, Alicia?"

"Cooking and contriving, Papa."

"What else have you been doing, Alicia?"

"Keeping the children lighthearted, Papa."

"Where is the magic fishbone, Alicia?"

"In my pocket, Papa."

131

"I thought you had lost it?"

"Oh, no, Papa!"

"Or forgotten it?"

"No, indeed, Papa."

The king then sighed so heavily, and seemed so low-spirited, and sat down so miserably, leaning his head upon his hand, that the seventeen princes and princesses crept softly out of the kitchen and left him alone with the Princess Alicia and the angelic baby.

"What is the matter, Papa?"

"I am dreadfully poor, my child."

"Have you no money at all, Papa?"

"None, my child."

"Is there no way of getting any, Papa?"

"No way," said the king. "I have tried very hard.

When she heard those last words, the Princess Alicia began to put her hand into the pocket where she kept the magic fishbone.

"Papa," said she. "When we have tried very hard, and tried all ways, we must have done our very, very best?"

"No doubt, Alicia."

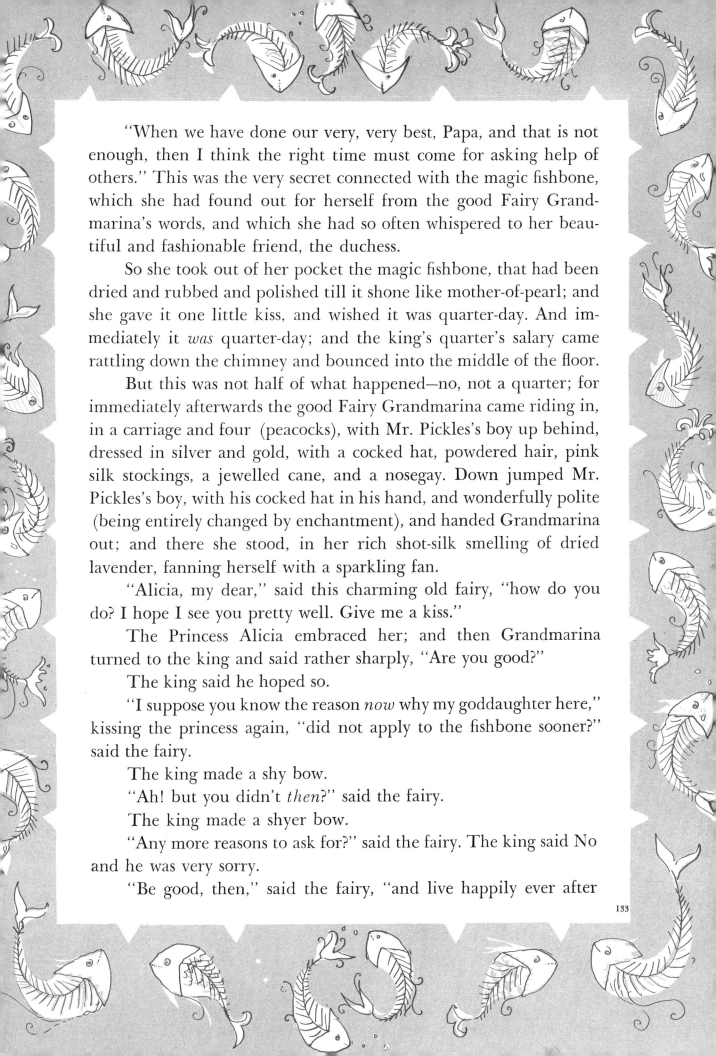

"When we have done our very, very best, Papa, and that is not enough, then I think the right time must come for asking help of others." This was the very secret connected with the magic fishbone, which she had found out for herself from the good Fairy Grandmarina's words, and which she had so often whispered to her beautiful and fashionable friend, the duchess.

So she took out of her pocket the magic fishbone, that had been dried and rubbed and polished till it shone like mother-of-pearl; and she gave it one little kiss, and wished it was quarter-day. And immediately it *was* quarter-day; and the king's quarter's salary came rattling down the chimney and bounced into the middle of the floor.

But this was not half of what happened—no, not a quarter; for immediately afterwards the good Fairy Grandmarina came riding in, in a carriage and four (peacocks), with Mr. Pickles's boy up behind, dressed in silver and gold, with a cocked hat, powdered hair, pink silk stockings, a jewelled cane, and a nosegay. Down jumped Mr. Pickles's boy, with his cocked hat in his hand, and wonderfully polite (being entirely changed by enchantment), and handed Grandmarina out; and there she stood, in her rich shot-silk smelling of dried lavender, fanning herself with a sparkling fan.

"Alicia, my dear," said this charming old fairy, "how do you do? I hope I see you pretty well. Give me a kiss."

The Princess Alicia embraced her; and then Grandmarina turned to the king and said rather sharply, "Are you good?"

The king said he hoped so.

"I suppose you know the reason *now* why my goddaughter here," kissing the princess again, "did not apply to the fishbone sooner?" said the fairy.

The king made a shy bow.

"Ah! but you didn't *then*?" said the fairy.

The king made a shyer bow.

"Any more reasons to ask for?" said the fairy. The king said No and he was very sorry.

"Be good, then," said the fairy, "and live happily ever after

133

Then Grandmarina waved her fan, and the queen came in most splendidly dressed; and the seventeen young princes and princesses, no longer grown out of their clothes, came in, newly fitted out from top to toe. After that, the fairy tapped the Princess Alicia with her fan; and the smothering coarse apron flew away, and she appeared exquisitely dressed, like a little bride, with a wreath of orange-flowers and a silver veil. After that, the kitchen dresser changed of itself into a wardrobe, made of beautiful woods and gold and looking-glass, which was full of dresses of all sorts, all for her and all exactly fitting her. After that, the angelic baby came running in alone, with his face and eye not a bit the worse, but much the better. Then Grandmarina begged to be introduced to the duchess; and, when the duchess was brought down, many compliments passed between them.

A little whispering took place between the fairy and the duchess; and then the fairy said out loud, "Yes, I thought she would have told you." Grandmarina then turned to the king and queen, and said, "We are going in search of Prince Certainpersonio. The pleasure of your company is requested at church in half an hour precisely." So she and the Princess Alicia got into the carriage; and Mr. Pickles's boy handed in the duchess, who sat by herself on the opposite seat; and then Mr. Pickles's boy put up the steps and got up behind, and the peacocks flew away with their tails behind.

Prince Certainpersonio was sitting by himself, eating barley-sugar, and waiting to be ninety.

When he saw the peacocks, followed by the carriage, coming in at the window, it immediately occurred to him that something uncommon was going to happen.

"Prince," said Grandmarina, "I bring you your bride."

The moment the fairy said those words, Prince Certainpersonio's face left off being sticky, and his jacket and corduroys changed to peach-bloom velvet, and his hair curled, and a cap and feather flew in like a bird and settled on his head. He got into the carriage by

the fairy's invitation; and there he renewed his acquaintance with the duchess, whom he had seen before.

In the church were the prince's relations and friends, and the Princess Alicia's relations and friends, and the seventeen princes and princesses, and the baby, and a crowd of the neighbors. The marriage was beautiful beyond expression. The duchess was bridesmaid, and beheld the ceremony from the pulpit, where she was supported by the cushion of the desk.

Grandmarina gave a magnificent wedding feast afterwards, in which there was everything and more to eat, and everything and more to drink. The wedding cake was delicately ornamented with white satin ribbons, frosted silver, and white lilies, and was forty-two yards round.

When Grandmarina had drunk her love to the young couple, and Prince Certainpersonio had made a speech, and everybody had cried, "Hip, hip, hip, hurrah!" Grandmarina announced to the king and queen that in the future there would be eight quarter-days in every year, except in leap year, when there would be ten. She then turned to Certainpersonio and Alicia and said, "My dears, you will have thirty-five children, and they will be all good and beautiful. Seventeen of your children will be boys, and eighteen will be girls. The hair of the whole of your children will curl naturally. They will never have the measles, and will have recovered from the whooping-cough before being born."

On hearing such good news, everybody cried out "Hip, hip, hip, hurrah!" again.

"It only remains," said Grandmarina in conclusion, "to make an end of the fishbone."

She she took it from the hand of the Princess Alicia, said a few magic words, and it vanished forever.

The Land
of Green Ginger

ILLUSTRATED BY WILLIAM BOLIN

YOU MUST HAVE HEARD HOW, in a time long ago in far-off China, a poor, ragged boy named Aladdin found a wonderful lamp; and how, when he accidentally rubbed the lamp, an enormous genie appeared, bound to serve him in every way and to fulfill his every wish.

With the help of his loyal genie, summoned by the lamp, Aladdin grew rich and powerful. As he was also wise and generous he was respected by all; and in the course of years he rose to be Emperor of all China. Now he lacked but one thing to make him happy: a good Queen to help him rule wisely and well. So once again he called the faithful genie to him, and with the genie's help he found a Princess who was as good as she was beautiful. As soon as he saw her he knew that she was to be his true love, and he made her his Queen.

"I shall ask no more happiness than this," said Aladdin, and in his gratitude he now gave the genie, Abdul, his freedom, promising to call upon him no more. To insure that the genie of the lamp would never again be called to serve any master, Aladdin caused the magic lamp to be placed in a separate room, where the most trusted of the Emperor's guards stood watch night and day. Orders were given that no one was ever to be allowed to touch it — not even the Emperor himself.

After a time a son was born to Aladdin, and as he grew to manhood the Emperor was pleased, for he saw that the Prince, Abu Ali, was both handsome and brave, a fitting heir to the throne of China. When the Prince came of age the Emperor began to think that it was time a suitable bride was found for him. So messengers were sent out, and the most beautiful princesses were brought from the far corners of the earth, and presented for his choice. But though he was courteous to them all, he found he could not love any of them; and he vowed that he would marry only one he could truly love. The Emperor was greatly troubled by this, for he knew that the Prince must marry or his succession to the throne would be endangered. At last, losing patience with his son's refusal, Aladdin commanded him to choose a bride from among the many princesses who had been presented. Abu Ali loved his father greatly, and had always obeyed him in all things; but in this he could not.

"Surely," he thought, "my true love must be somewhere. If only I could find her my father would not force me to marry any other!" But where should he seek for her?

Then, in his desperation, he remembered that the powerful genie of the lamp had helped his father to find his dearly loved Queen. Perhaps the genie would help him, too. But to touch the lamp was forbidden, even to the Emperor's son. He had been warned that the genie, if disturbed, might destroy anyone who called him back from his freedom. But now Abu Ali felt he must risk this, and his father's anger, too. It was his only hope.

When Abu Ali went to the room where the magic lamp was kept, the guard saluted him respectfully. The Prince addressed him in friendly tones: "Let me take over your watch for a while," he said. "Perhaps you would like to stretch your legs for a few moments."

"That cannot be, Your Highness," the guard replied. "My duty is to remain here."

Abu Ali tried again. Moving closer to the lamp and looking at it eagerly, he said: "Do you not think someone ought to polish that old lamp?"

But the guard, now thoroughly alarmed, placed himself between the lamp and Abu Ali. "Your Highness knows that no one is permitted to touch the lamp!"

Then, throwing all caution to the winds, Abu Ali brushed the guard aside and seized the lamp. The terrified guard, not daring to strike the Emperor's son, rushed off shouting for the Emperor himself to come.

Now that Abu Ali had the lamp in his hands he was suddenly afraid. Perhaps the terrible genie would throw him into the sea for disobeying his father's orders. But he knew that Abdul had loved his father greatly; might he not then understand the son's great need? He rubbed the lamp timidly, and waited. Nothing happened. Then, growing bolder, he rubbed it more vigorously. Instantly there was a crash as of thunder, and a blinding light. A spiral of smoke curled upward from the floor and, as it cleared, the mighty genie, Abdul, stood before him, glaring down at him fiercely.

"Who dares call me from my freedom?" he demanded angrily.

"It is I, Abu Ali, son of Aladdin," said the Prince, as bravely as he could.

"By what right do you break Aladdin's promise?" thundered the genie.

"Mighty Genie," said the Prince, "for the love you bore my father, I beg you to hear me."

"Did you not know that your father gave me my freedom and promised I would never be called again to serve a mortal man?"

"Yes, mighty Abdul," the Prince replied, "I know. And I will not keep you for long. I want only to ask you one question."

"Very well, young Master. Be brief," said Abdul.

"I am in deep trouble," Abu Ali told him. "My father wishes me to marry."

"It is right that the Prince should marry," Abdul said gravely.

"Yes," cried Abu Ali. "But among all the princesses my father has brought for my choosing, I do not find one I truly love, and I cannot marry any other. Somewhere in the wide world there must be one who is my true love! Can you not help me find her as you helped my father find my beloved mother?"

The genie was silent for a moment. Then he said:

"Your request is fair. Yes, just this once, I will help Aladdin's son."

Now he began a low chant, invoking the spirits of the future to grant Abu Ali's wish to see his true love. A gentle wind sprang up, blowing a mist before the Prince's eyes. And then, slowly, in the mist, Abu Ali saw, as in a mirror, a beautiful princess who sat combing her

hair. In her blue eyes beneath her clear brow there was a look of wonderment and questioning, as if she, too, were searching for some-one.

Abu Ali gazed at her a long time in silence. Then . . .

"Are you answered?" asked Abdul gruffly.

"Yes—oh yes," the Prince answered, overwhelmed by this vision of pure loveliness. Then as the picture slowly dissolved in the mist, he cried: "She is gone! What is her name? Where shall I find her?"

"Her name is Silverbud," Abdul replied. "Her father is King of Samarkand. You will find her there."

"I must go at once," said the Prince eagerly. "I shall ask my father to send a great caravan to bring her here, as befits the future bride of the Emperor's son."

"Not so fast, Prince!" warned Abdul. "The Princess Silverbud also wishes to marry only one she truly loves. You will win her hand only if she loves you for yourself. Not until you have won her heart may you tell her that you are the son of Aladdin, heir to the throne of China."

"Great Abdul," said Abu Ali, "will you not guide me to Samarkand?"

"That cannot be," said the genie. "You must go alone. But one thing I will promise. Know this, Abu Ali! If you are ever in dire peril, once, *and once only*, you may rub the lamp again, and I will come. Beyond that I can promise nothing! Bear yourself wisely. Farewell!"

And the genie vanished, as he had come, in a curl of smoke and a clap of thunder.

The Prince then begged leave of his father to set out at once, and Aladdin consented, though he would have wished to send his son to seek his bride with more pomp and splendor. But Abu Ali insisted that he must go alone and unknown, and he would take only his trusted donkey to carry him. In this fashion, and garbed as an ordinary traveler, he set out to seek the land of Samarkand, and win the love of the Princess Silverbud.

Many days he traveled. His sure-footed donkey took him safely over rough mountain passes and through tangled woods and dense forests. At last he found himself at the edge of the desert that lay between the mountains and the land of Samarkand. All day donkey and rider made their way across the trackless sand under a blazing sun. Toward evening Abu Ali was happy to see in the distance the leafy tops of trees that shaded an oasis, and he hurried his donkey toward it. As he came near he saw that two caravans of men and camels were already encamped there. Soon he was close enough to hear voices. The two men who, to all appearances, were the owners of the caravans, seemed to be quarreling violently. Not particularly interested in the cause of their quarrel, Abu Ali rounded the rocky ledge which had hidden him from their view, and came into the pleasant shade of the oasis.

"Good evening," he said.

The men glared at him with unfriendly eyes. One of them asked roughly: "Who are you? Why are you here?"

"Just a tired traveler, on my way to Samarkand," Abu Ali replied truthfully. "I wish only to pass the night in this cool spot, and will be off again at sunrise." And he began to prepare a place to sleep beside his donkey.

The two men drew aside, talking in low tones, and Abu Ali had a disquieting feeling that they were plotting something that boded him no good. However, very soon they fell to quarreling with each other again, their voices rising angrily. And now Abu Ali learned, to his distress, that these two middle-aged princes were both on their way to Samarkand to woo the Princess Silverbud. They were quarreling about which of them had the best right to claim her hand. Their discovery that this handsome young traveler was also bound for Samarkand had thrown them into a frenzy. Now, added to their rivalry with each other, was their common need to keep this young fellow from reaching the Princess before they did. While they were bitterly wrangling over what was to be done and which of them was to do it, Abu Ali quietly mounted his donkey and rode off toward Samarkand. It was some time before they discovered his absence.

Meanwhile in Samarkand, the King had prepared his daughter to receive the two princely suitors who were coming to seek her hand in marriage.

"Are they kind, handsome and considerate?" the gentle Princess asked.

"I do not know about that," her father replied. "But they are both princes, and they are both rich." Either would be a suitable husband for his daughter, he told her, and she must make her choice between them. "I must ride out to meet them. Go now and have your attendants dress you in your loveliest robes, and come to the palace gates to bid them welcome."

Poor Silverbud! What could she do but wait helplessly for a fate that was to be decided for her? As she came slowly and unwillingly forward toward the palace gate where she was to await the approaching suitors, she sighed and murmured, half-aloud:

"What shall I do if I can love neither of these princes? I would rather die than marry a man I do not truly love!"

As if in answer to her cry of despair, suddenly Abu Ali stood before her in the open gateway. Softly he said, "Ah, Silverbud, those are the very words I hoped to hear you say!"

The Princess looked at him in startled surprise. "How did you come here—and how do you know my name?"

"I know your name by the magic of this lamp," the Prince replied; "the same magic that made me love you even before this moment of our meeting. But you are even more beautiful than my vision!"

"Your vision?" she asked. "Where do you come from? Who are you?"

"My name is Abu Ali. But that is all I may tell you."

Now she saw her father coming toward them, and at his side were the two princes who had ridden in from the desert with their caravans. As they came closer the King frowned when he saw Abu Ali standing by the side of the Princess.

"Who is this?" he asked his daughter angrily.

Before she could answer, the two suitors hurriedly declared that this young man was a low-born, thieving fellow they had met on their journey. For the protection of the Princess and the King, they urged, he should be seized at once and put to death. But when the guards would have laid hold of Abu Ali the Princess placed herself in front of him.

"Do not dare to touch him!" she said. "For I must tell you—if I do not marry him, I will marry no one!"

Her father was in despair. "Do you not understand, my daughter?" he said. "This man is not a prince of royal blood. How do we know that he is worthy to marry a king's daughter?"

Now Abu Ali came forward to the King, and said:

"Sir, I beg of you to set a task for me—for all three of us. Then the Princess can judge for herself which of us is the bravest and the most worthy of her."

At this one of the two suitors whispered something in the ear of the King, who smiled cunningly and said:

"It shall be as you say. We will set this task for you: you will bring back to us three tail feathers from the magic Phoenix Bird. Do not return here without them!"

"But, my father," Silverbud cried. "That is impossible! There have been no Phoenix Birds in this land since they disappeared many years ago."

"That may be as it may," said the King. "But this young man may not return here unless he brings with him the three feathers we demanded. And now you, yourself, my Silverbud, shall set the trials for the two royal princes."

"Very well," said the Princess. And turning to the reluctant princes she said: "You will each bring to me a magic carpet. And be sure it is one that flies at its master's command."

The two princes would gladly have remained at their ease, entertained at the King's palace. But since each hoped to win the Princess Silverbud, and fall heir to her father's spacious kingdom, they had now no choice but to set out on the quest the Princess had

set for them. Though they still hated each other, they felt they must
first work together to rid themselves of their common enemy, Abu
Ali. So, since the way might be perilous, they agreed to set out together in their search for two magic carpets to please the Princess.

Meanwhile, Abu Ali had lost no time in setting out on his donkey. For many long, weary hours he traveled over land that was
strange to him. Many times the donkey faltered and turned aside
from rough paths which his instinct told him might be dangerous.
But along the way they met neither man nor beast. At last, toward
nightfall, they came into a dark and gloomy forest. The donkey
hesitated to enter, but the cooling trees seemed to offer a shelter for
the night, and Abu Ali led the donkey to a small clearing not far
into the forest, and prepared to rest here until daybreak. He was
about to tether the animal to a tree, when out from behind it a mov-

ing shape came slowly toward him. His feet froze to the spot as the dark form became clearer, and he saw that it was a dragon. The donkey pulled wildly at its tether. However, the dragon seemed gentle enough, and Abu Ali stood his ground and waited. Then, in a friendly voice, the creature addressed him, asking what he sought in the forest.

"I have come to find the magic Phoenix Bird," Abu Ali said politely.

"Ah," said the dragon, "that will not be easy, for the Phoenix Bird no longer lives in this land. There is only one place where you will find him, and you cannot go there."

"What is that place?" Abu Ali asked.

"He lives now in the Land of Green Ginger," the dragon told him.

"And can you not tell me where I may find that land?" asked Abu Ali eagerly.

"You will have to wait until it finds you," replied the dragon. "For the Land of Green Ginger is an enchanted country. It comes and goes and moves about, and never remains long in one place. It is impossible to know where it will be at any time."

"Thank you," said Abu Ali. "But I must find it!"

"Very well," said the dragon, "but you will have to go on foot, for I am hungry, and I have a mind to eat your donkey for my dinner."

Abu Ali was horrified. "That you shall not do!" he cried. And as the dragon moved forward with outstretched claws, he quickly loosed the tether and slapped the faithful donkey briskly on its flank, and the frightened animal galloped away, glad to have this order from his master to leave that dread place.

Now the dragon roared in anger: "He is gone, but *you* are still here. I shall eat you instead."

In his extreme peril, Abu Ali remembered the genie's promise to respond once to the call of the lamp. Surely he would never need the help of Abdul more than now! With a quick motion he pulled the lamp from his belt and rubbed it. Instantly there was a loud clap of thunder, and then a tall curl of smoke rose from the ground. Terrified, the dragon plunged off into the forest, and Abu Ali could hear him trampling down the forest undergrowth in his haste. Then the sound died in the distance. Now Abu Ali waited, watching the curl of smoke. But instead of the mighty Abdul there came out of it a small, fat genie, about three and a half feet high.

"What . . . Who are you?" asked Abu Ali in surprise.

"I am Abdul's son, Boomalakka Wee. When your call came, and I saw that my father was sleeping, I came instead. You see, you did not rub the lamp hard enough to bring my father. I know I am very small, but I will do my best to serve you. What is your wish?"

"You are indeed very small to perform magic," said Abu Ali. "Yet I hope you can bring me the one thing that I need: a donkey to carry me to the Land of Green Ginger, where I may find the magic Phoenix Bird."

The small genie raised his arm, and began to chant a charm. A tiny gray cloud rolled to their feet, and out of it came a small but angry mouse.

"I'm sorry," said Boomalakka Wee. "I *did* ask for a donkey. But it's because I am so small—I can only make small things come. Now I don't know how to send it back, so we will have to go on foot, and take the mouse along. And you never know when a mouse may serve your need."

"Well," said Abu Ali, "we must make the best of it. Only I do not know in what direction to go to find the Land of Green Ginger. Perhaps, since it is a magic land, we might bring it here if we all wish hard enough."

So they sat on the ground for a few moments, sending silent wishes for the enchanted land to come to this spot. After a while, Abu Ali put his wish into words, and called aloud to the Land of Green Ginger. Suddenly they found themselves enveloped by a strange mist. Then they realized that the ground on which they were sitting was covered with soft grass. As the mist slowly cleared,

Abu Ali saw that the grass under his feet was very green, and beautiful flowers and leafy trees were growing all around them. And then he saw, standing in a clearing among the trees, and almost as big as the trees themselves, two great, fierce-looking Phoenix Birds. They stood facing each other, preening their feathers, and from time to time pecking angrily at one another.

How could he dare to pluck these fierce birds? But as Abu Ali watched their angry attacks on one another, an idea came to him. He hid himself among the bushes, and tore off two long, stiff palm branches. Then, reaching out from his hiding place, he struck one of the birds with the hard, prickly branch. The furious bird, believing that the other had attacked it, rushed upon it, beating with its huge wings, and plucked out several of its straight tail feathers. With a piercing shriek the injured bird pursued its attacker, and both soared out of sight with a loud flapping of wings.

Abu Ali rushed from his hiding place, and gathered three of the tall white feathers from the ground. "Now I go to claim the Princess Silverbud," he shouted, happily.

But as he spoke the two rival princes burst upon him and ordered their servants to seize and bind him. The two suitors had been able to find only one magic carpet between them. Neither would let the other ride upon it, for each claimed he owned it and would present it to the Princess. And since they had been obliged to barter their camels for the carpet, they had been forced to walk carrying the precious carpet between them. They had lost their way, and had stumbled onto the Land of Green Ginger without knowing it. And now they found they had their rival in their power. They would make sure that he did not return to Samarkand.

One of the servants snatched the three feathers from the now helpless Abu Ali, and another picked up the lamp. He looked at it doubtfully, and was about to throw it down, but decided to make off with it, though it appeared to be an old, battered and worthless thing. Leaving Abu Ali firmly bound and unable to move, the men continued on their journey to claim the unhappy Princess for whichever of them she would choose.

As soon as they were out of sight the little mouse busied herself among the ropes which bound Abu Ali, and before long had gnawed enough to free his hands so that he might get loose from the rest.

"We must go after them at once, for I must get back the three feathers," he called to the small genie.

"Give me the magic lamp," said Boomalakka Wee. "Perhaps if *I* rub the lamp my father, the great Abdul, will come to help us."

And now, for the first time, Abu Ali saw that the precious lamp was gone. At the same moment he felt that the ground under his feet was swaying. It was moving upward into the air, and all three of them were being lifted with it. The Land of Green Ginger was moving, they did not know to where.

When the two scheming princes reached the land of Samarkand,

they presented themselves to the King, and laid the magic carpet at the feet of the Princess.

"Now, my daughter," the King said, "you must choose a husband between these two."

But Silverbud said: "I will not choose until Abu Ali returns."

"Ah, Princess, I fear that will never be," said one of the princes, with a pretense at great sadness, "for he was eaten by a dragon in the forest."

"See," added the other prince, "we found these few of his possessions left on the ground, for the dragon had not been able to eat them: these three feathers of the magic Phoenix Bird, and this old lamp."

"That lamp—give me that lamp," cried Silverbud.

Seizing it from the servant who carried it, she clasped it excitedly and said softly: "Magic lamp, bring Abu Ali back to me!"

"Look!" cried one of the caravan guards, pointing to the distant sky. What appeared to be a large, dark cloud was coming rapidly

154

toward them sailing crazily among the other clouds. "A terrible thunder storm is coming, and it is almost upon us."

"No," said Princess Silverbud, "that is no thunder cloud, for see, it is covered with grass and trees. The magic lamp has brought the Land of Green Ginger here to us. Perhaps it brings us news of Abu Ali."

As the green land came to rest before the palace gates, Abu Ali and his friends, Boomalakka Wee and the mouse, jumped from it into the garden where the Princess was standing with her father.

"Seize that man," shouted the King. But before the guards could obey his command, the small genie snatched the lamp from the Princess's trembling hands and rubbed it violently. There was a clap of thunder, and a dense curl of smoke rose from the ground. When it cleared, there, before the terrified eyes of all, stood the mighty genie, Abdul. He glared down at the two quaking princes for a long moment, then, turning to Abu Ali, he said sternly: "I promised you one wish, young master. What is your will? And what shall I do with these two rogues?"

The two princes now fell on their knees and begged Abu Ali not to have them punished. But the young Prince brushed them aside, and taking the hand of the Princess went with her to her father.

"I wish only the King's consent to take the Princess Silverbud home to my own land as my bride," he said.

"But who are you—and where is your home?" asked the King, trembling with fear.

"Know ye all," thundered Abdul, "that this is His Royal Highness Prince Abu Ali, son of the great Emperor Aladdin, and heir to the throne of China."

Now the King was overcome with relief and joy, and readily gave his consent. The marriage was celebrated at once. After a great feast in the palace, Abu Ali led his Princess to the edge of the Land of Green Ginger. As they stepped up onto its grassy lawn from the palace garden the magic land slowly rose into the air, and flew like a gentle breeze into the distant sky, off toward the land of China.

The Emperor's New Clothes

ILLUSTRATED BY JOHN ALCORN

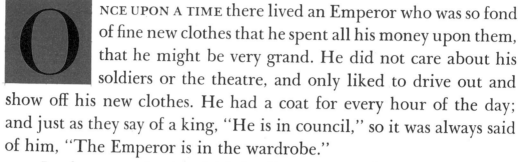

O NCE UPON A TIME there lived an Emperor who was so fond of fine new clothes that he spent all his money upon them, that he might be very grand. He did not care about his soldiers or the theatre, and only liked to drive out and show off his new clothes. He had a coat for every hour of the day; and just as they say of a king, "He is in council," so it was always said of him, "The Emperor is in the wardrobe."

In the great city in which he lived many strangers came every day. One day two rogues came. They said they were weavers, and declared they could weave the finest stuff anyone could imagine. Not only were their colors and patterns uncommonly beautiful, they said, but the clothes made of the stuff possessed the wonderful quality that they became invisible to anyone who was unfit for the office he held or was very stupid.

"Those would be most unusual clothes!" thought the Emperor. "If I wore those, I should be able to find out what men in my empire are not fit for the places they have; I could tell the clever ones from the dunces. Yes, the stuff must be woven for me directly!"

And he gave the two rogues a great deal of cash, so that they might begin their work at once.

As for them, they put up two looms, and pretended to be working; but they had nothing at all on their looms. They at once demanded the finest silk and the costliest gold; this they put into their own pockets, and worked at the empty looms till late into the night.

A few weeks passed. Then the Emperor said to himself, "I should like to know how far they have got on with the stuff." But he felt quite uncomfortable when he thought that those who were not fit for their offices could not see it. He believed, of course, that he had nothing to fear for himself, but he preferred first to send someone else to see how matters stood.

"I will send my honest old Minister to the weavers," thought the Emperor. "He can judge best how the stuff looks, for he has sense, and no one understands his office better than he."

So the good old Minister went out into the hall where the two rogues sat working at the empty looms.

"Mercy on us!" thought the old Minister, and he opened his eyes wide. "I cannot see anything at all! Can I indeed be so stupid? I never thought that, and not a soul must know it. Am I not fit for my office? No, it will never do for me to tell that I could not see the stuff."

"Haven't you anything to say about it?" asked one of the rogues, as he went on weaving. "O, it is charming — quite enchanting!" answered the old Minister, as he peered through his spectacles. "What a fine pattern, and what colors! Yes, I shall tell the Emperor that I am very much pleased with it."

Now the rogues asked for more money, and silk and gold, which they declared they wanted for weaving. They put it all into their own pockets, and not a thread was put upon the loom; they continued to work at the empty frames as before.

The Emperor soon sent another honest officer of the court to see how the weaving was going on, and if the stuff would soon be ready. He fared just like the first: he looked and looked, but, as there was nothing to be seen but the empty looms, he could see nothing.

"Isn't that a pretty piece of stuff?" asked the two rogues; and they displayed and explained the handsome pattern which was not there at all.

"I am not stupid!" thought the man. "Yet it must be that I am not fit for my office. If that is the case, I must not let it be noticed." And so he praised the stuff which he did not see, and expressed his pleasure at the beautiful colors and charming pattern. "Yes, it is enchanting," he told the Emperor.

All the people in the town were talking of the gorgeous stuff. The Emperor wished to see it himself while it was still upon the loom.

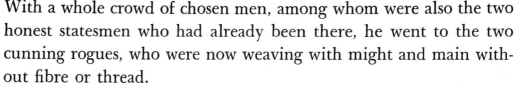

With a whole crowd of chosen men, among whom were also the two honest statesmen who had already been there, he went to the two cunning rogues, who were now weaving with might and main without fibre or thread.

"Isn't that splendid?" said the two statesmen, who had already been there once. "Doesn't your Majesty approve of the pattern and the colors?" And they pointed to the empty loom, for they thought that the others could see the stuff.

"What's this?" thought the Emperor. "I can see nothing at all! That is terrible. Am I stupid? Am I not fit to be Emperor? That would be the most dreadful thing that could happen to me. O, it is *very* pretty!" he said aloud. "It has our highest approval." And he nodded in a contented way, and gazed at the empty loom, for he would not say that he saw nothing. Those whom he had with him looked and looked, and saw nothing, any more than the rest; but, like the Emperor, they said, "That *is* pretty!" and advised him to wear the splendid new clothes for the first time at the great procession that was to take place the following week. "It is splendid, excellent!" went from mouth to mouth. On all sides there seemed to be general rejoicing, and the Emperor gave the rogues the title of Imperial Court Weavers.

The whole night before the morning on which the procession was to take place, the rogues were up, keeping more than sixteen candles burning. The people could see that they were hard at work, completing the Emperor's new clothes. They pretended to take the stuff down from the loom: they made great slashes in the air with their scissors; they sewed with needles without thread; and at last they said, "Now the clothes are ready!"

The Emperor came himself with his noblest cavaliers; and the two rogues lifted their arms as if they were holding something, and said, "See, here are the trousers! here is the coat! here is the cloak!" and so on. "It is as light as a spider's web: one would think one had nothing on; but that is just the beauty of it."

"Yes," said all the cavaliers; but they could not see anything, for nothing was there.

"Will your Imperial Majesty please take off your clothes?" said the rogues. "Then we will put on you the new clothes here in front of the great mirror."

The Emperor took off his clothes, and the rogues pretended to put on him each new garment as it was ready; and the Emperor turned round and round before the mirror.

"O, how fine they look! how well they fit!" said everybody. "What a pattern! what colors! That *is* a splendid outfit."

"They are standing outside with the canopy which is to be borne above your Majesty in the procession!" announced the Master of the Ceremonies.

"Well, I am ready," replied the Emperor. "Does it not suit me well?" And then he turned again to the mirror, for he wanted it to appear as if he contemplated his adornment with great interest.

The two chamberlains who were to carry the train stooped down

with their hands toward the floor, just as if they were picking up the mantle; then they pretended to be holding something in the air.

So the Emperor went in procession under the rich canopy, and everyone in the streets said, "How elegant are the Emperor's new clothes! What a train he has to his mantle! How it fits him!" No one would let it be known that he could see nothing, for that would have shown that he was not fit for his office, or was very stupid.

"But he has nothing on!" a little child cried out at last.

"Just hear what the innocent says!" said the father. And each person began whispering to another what the child had said.

"But he has nothing on!" said all the people at last. That touched the Emperor, for it seemed to him that they were right; but he thought to himself, "I must go through with the procession." And so he held himself a little higher, and the chamberlains held on tighter than ever, and carried the train which did not exist at all.

The Valiant Little Tailor

ILLUSTRATED BY GERTRUDE ELLIOTT ESPENSCHEID

A TAILOR SAT in his workroom one morning, stitching away busily at a coat for the Lord Mayor.

"How hungry I feel, to be sure!" cried the little man, at last; "but I'm far too busy to trouble about eating. I must finish his lordship's coat before I touch a morsel of food." And he broke into a merry song.

"Fine new jam for sale," sang out an old woman, as she walked along the street.

"Jam! I can't resist such a treat," said the tailor; and, running to the door, he shouted: "This way for jam, dame; show me a pot of your very finest and I'll take four ounces."

"Now for a feed!" cried the little man, taking a loaf from the cupboard as he spoke. He cut off a huge slice, and spread the jam on quite half an inch thick; then he suddenly remembered his work.

"It will never do to get jam on the Lord Mayor's coat, so I'll finish it off before I take even one bite," said he. So he picked up his work once more, and his needle flew in and out like lightning.

The tailor glanced longingly at his slice of bread and jam once or twice, but when he looked the third time it was quite covered with flies enjoying the fine feast.

This was too much for the little fellow. Up he jumped, crying: "So you think I provide bread and jam for you, indeed! Well, we'll very soon see! Take that!" and he struck the flies such a heavy blow with a duster that no fewer than seven lay dead upon the table, while the others flew up to the ceiling in great haste.

"Seven at one blow!" said the little man with great pride. "Such a brave deed ought to be known all over the town, and it won't be my fault if folks fail to hear of it."

So he cut out a wide belt, and stitched on it in big golden letters the words "Seven at one blow." When this was done he fastened it round him, crying: "I'm cut out for something better than a tailor, it's quite clear. I'm one of the world's great heroes, and I'll be off at once to seek my fortune."

He glanced round the cottage, but there was nothing of value to take with him. The only thing he possessed in the world was a small cheese. "You may as well come, too," said he, stowing away the cheese in his pocket, "and now I'm off."

He jogged along for some miles until he came to a hedge, where a little bird was caught in the branches. "Come along," said the tailor; "I'll have you to keep my cheese company;" so he caught the bird and put it carefully into his pocket with the cheese.

Soon he reached a lofty mountain, and he made up his mind to climb it and see what was going on at the other side. When he reached the top, there stood a huge giant gazing down into the valley below.

"Good day," said the tailor.

The giant turned round, and seeing nobody but the little tailor there, he cried with scorn: "And what might you be doing here might I ask? You'd best be off at once."

"Not so fast, my friend," said the little man; "read this."

"Seven at one blow," read the giant, and he began to wish he'd been more civil.

"Well, I'm sure nobody would think it to look at you," he replied; "but since you are so clever, do this," and he picked up a stone and squeezed it until water ran out.

"Do that! Why, it's mere child's play to me," and the tailor took out his cheese and squeezed it until the whey ran from it. "Now who is cleverer?" he asked. "You see, I can squeeze milk out, while you only get water."

The giant was too surprised to utter a word for a few minutes; then, taking up another stone, he threw it so high into the air that for a moment they couldn't see where it went; then down it fell to the ground again.

"Good!" said the tailor. "But I'll throw a stone that won't come back at all."

Taking the little bird from his pocket, he threw it into the air, and the bird, glad to get away, flew right off and never returned.

This sort of thing didn't suit the giant at all, for he wasn't used to being beaten by anyone.

"Here's something that you'll never manage," said he to the little man. "Just come and help me to carry this fallen oak tree for a few miles."

"Delighted!" said the tailor. "And I'll take the end with the branches, for it's sure to be heavier."

"Agreed," replied the giant, and he lifted the heavy trunk onto his shoulder, while the tailor climbed up among the branches at the other end, and sang with all his might, as though carrying a tree was nothing to him.

The poor giant, who was holding the treetrunk and the little tailor as well, soon grew tired.

"I'm going to let it fall!" he shouted, and the tailor jumped down from the branches, and pretended he had been helping all the time.

"The idea of a man your size finding a tree too heavy to carry!" said the little tailor, laughing.

"You are a clever little fellow, and no mistake," replied the giant, "and if you'll only come and spend the night in our cave, we shall be delighted to have you."

"I shall have great pleasure in coming, my friend," answered the little tailor, and together they set off for the giant's home.

There were seven more giants in the cave, and each one of them was eating a roasted pig for his supper. They gave the little man some food, and then showed him a bed in which he might pass the

night. It was so big that, after tossing about for half an hour in it, the tailor thought he would be more comfortable if he slept in the corner, so he crept out without being noticed.

In the middle of the night the giant stole out of bed and went up to the one where he thought the little man was fast asleep. Taking a big bar of iron, he struck such a heavy blow at it that he woke up all the other giants.

"Keep quiet, friends," said he. "I've just killed the little scamp."

The tailor made his escape as soon as possible, and he journeyed on for many miles, until he began to feel very tired. So he lay down under a tree, and was soon fast asleep.

When he awoke, he found a big crowd of people standing round him. Up walked one very wise-looking old man, who was really the king's prime minister.

"Is it true that you killed seven at one blow?" he asked.

"It is a fact," answered the little tailor.

"Then come with me to the king, my friend, for he's been searching for a brave man like you for some time past. You are to be made captain of his army, and the king will give you a fine house to live in."

"That I will," replied the little man. "It is just the sort of thing that will suit me, and I'll come at once."

He hadn't been in the king's service long before everyone grew jealous of him. The soldiers were afraid that if they offended him he would make short work of them all, while the members of the king's household didn't like the idea of making such a fuss over a stranger.

So the soldiers went in a body to the king and asked that another captain should be put over them, for they were afraid of this one.

The king didn't like to refuse for fear they should all desert, and yet he didn't dare get rid of the captain, for so strong and brave a man might try to have his revenge.

At last the king hit upon a plan. In some woods close by there lived two giants who were the terror of the countryside; they robbed all the travelers, and if any resistance was offered they killed the men on the spot.

Sending for the little tailor, the king said:

"Knowing you to be the bravest man in my kingdom, I want to ask a favor of you. If you will kill these two giants, and bring me back proof that they are dead, you shall marry the princess, my daughter, and have half my kingdom. You shall also take one hundred men to help you, and you are to set off at once."

"A hundred men, your majesty! Pray, what do I want with a hundred men? If I can kill seven at one blow, I needn't be afraid of two. I'll kill them fast enough, never fear."

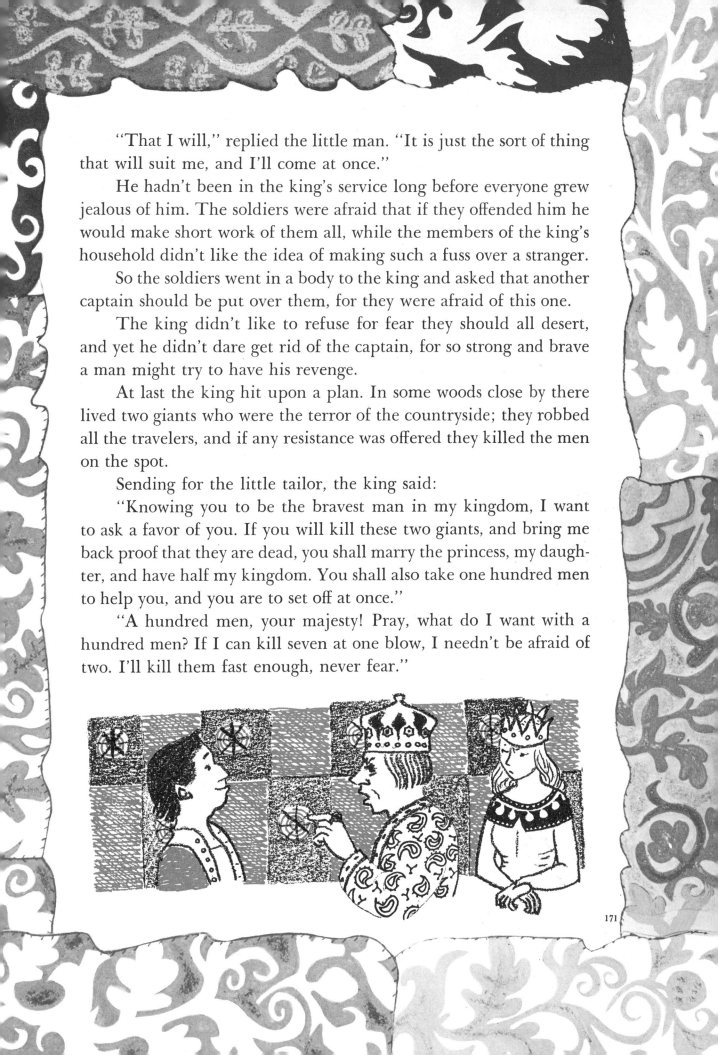

171

The tailor chose ten strong men, and told them to wait for him on the border of the wood while he went on quite alone. He could hear the giants snoring for quite half an hour before he reached them, so he knew in which direction to go.

He found the pair fast asleep under a tree, so he filled his pockets with stones and climbed up into the branches over their heads. Then he began to pelt one of the giants with the stones, until after a few minutes he awoke. Giving the other a rough push, he cried:

"If you strike me like that again, I'll know the reason why."

"I didn't touch you," said the other giant crossly, and they were soon fast asleep once more.

Then the tailor threw stones at the other giant, and soon he awoke as the first had done.

"Why did you throw that at me?" said he.

"You are dreaming," answered the other. "I didn't throw anything."

No sooner were they fast asleep again, than the little tailor began to pelt them afresh.

Up they both sprang and, seizing each other, they began to fight in real earnest. Not content with using their fists, they tore up huge trees by the roots, and beat each other until very soon the pair lay dead on the ground.

Down climbed the little tailor, and taking his sword in his hand he plunged it into each giant. Then he went back to the edge of the forest where the ten men were waiting for him.

"They are as dead as two door nails," shouted the little tailor. "I don't say that I had an easy task, for they tore up trees by their roots to try to protect themselves, but, of course, it was no good. What are two giants to a man who has slain seven at one blow?"

But the men wouldn't believe it until they went into the forest and saw the two dead bodies, lying in a pool of blood, while the ground was covered with uprooted trees.

Back they went to the king, but instead of handing over half his kingdom, as he had promised, his majesty told the little tailor that there was still another brave deed for him to do before he could have the princess for his bride.

"Just name it, then; I'm more than ready," was the little tailor's reply.

"You are to kill the famous unicorn that is running wild in the forest and doing so much damage. When this is done you shall have your reward at once."

"No trouble at all, your majesty. I'll get rid of him in a twinkling."

He made the ten men wait for him at the entrance to the wood, as they had done the first time and, taking a stout rope and a saw, he entered the forest alone.

Up came the unicorn, but just as it was about to rush at the little tailor he darted behind a big tree. The unicorn dashed with such force against the tree that its horn was caught quite fast and it was kept a prisoner. Taking his rope, the little tailor tied it tightly round the animal, and, after sawing off the horn, went back to the palace leading the unicorn by his side.

But even then the king was not satisfied, and he made the little tailor catch a wild boar that had been seen wandering in the woods. This time he took a party of huntsmen with him, but again he made them wait on the outskirts of the forest while he went on by himself.

The wild boar made a dash at the little tailor, but he was too quick for it. He slipped into a little building close by, with the animal at his heels. Then, catching sight of a small window, he forced his way out into the forest again. While the boar, who was too big and clumsy to follow, stood gazing at the spot where he had disappeared, the tailor ran around and closed the door, keeping the animal quite secure inside. Then he called the hunters, who shot the boar and carried the body back to the palace.

This time the king was obliged to keep his promise; so the little tailor became a prince, and there was a grand wedding, too.

One night, when they had been married for a couple of years, the princess overheard her husband talking in his sleep.

"Boys, if you have put a patch on that waistcoat, take the Lord Mayor's coat home at once, or I'll box your ears," he said.

"Oh dear," cried the princess, "to think that I've married a common tailor! Whatever can I do to get rid of him?"

So the next morning she told her father the story, and the king said she need not worry, for he would find a way out of the difficulty. She was to leave the door open that night and while the tailor was sleeping, the king's servants would steal into the room, bind the tailor, and take him away to be killed.

The princess promised to see that everything was in readiness, and she tripped about all day with a very light heart. She little knew that one of the tailor's servants had overheard the cruel plot and carried the news straight to his master.

That night, when the princess thought her husband was fast asleep, she crept to the door and opened it. To her great terror, the tailor began to speak.

"Boy, take the Lord Mayor's coat home, or I'll box your ears. Haven't I killed seven at one blow? Haven't I slain two giants, a unicorn, and a wild boar? What do I care for the men who are standing outside my door at this moment?"

At these words off flew the men as though they had been shot from a gun, and no more attempts were ever made on the little tailor's life. So the princess had to make the best of a bad job.

The little tailor lived on, and when the old king died, he ascended the throne in his stead, becoming ruler over the whole kingdom. And his motto throughout his whole life was, "Seven at one blow."

THE WILD SWANS 177

The Wild Swans

ILLUSTRATED BY TOM O'SULLIVAN

F AR AWAY, in a land where the swallows fly when our winter comes, there once lived a King who had eleven sons and one daughter. The eleven brothers—the young Princes—went to school each with a star on his breast and a sword at his side. They wrote upon slates of gold with pencils of diamond, and learned to say their lessons by heart as if they were reading them from a book; one could see that they were Princes. Their sister Elise sat upon a little glass stool, and had a picture-book which cost half a kingdom. Oh, these children had a happy time, but it was not to remain so.

Their father, who was King of the whole country, married a wicked Queen who did not love his poor children at all. On the very first day they knew this. In the Palace there was great feasting; but the children, instead of getting all the cakes and roasted apples they could eat, as they used to do, were only given some sand in a teacup, and told they might pretend it was something good.

The next week, the Queen took little Elise into the country to a peasant and his wife; and it was not long before the wicked Queen had told the King so many falsehoods about the poor Princes that he did not trouble himself about them any more.

"Fly out into the world and get your own living," the wicked Queen told the Princes. "Fly like great birds without a voice." But she could not do all the harm she had intended, for the Princes turned into eleven beautiful white swans. With a strange cry they flew out of the Palace windows, far over the park and into the wood.

It was still quite early morning when they came by the place where their sister Elise lay asleep in the peasant's house. Here they hovered over the roof, turned their long necks, and flapped their wings, but no one heard or saw them. They had to fly on, high up towards the clouds, far away into the wide world, and into a great dark wood which stretched away to the seashore.

Poor little Elise was standing in the peasant's house playing with a green leaf, for she had no other playthings. She picked a hole in the leaf, and looked through it up at the sun, and it seemed to her that she saw her brothers' clear eyes. When the warm sun shone on her cheeks, she remembered their kisses.

Each day passed just like the rest. When the wind swept through the rose bushes outside the house, it whispered to the roses, "Could anyone be more beautiful than you?" Then the roses answered, "Yes, Elise!" And on Sundays, when the old peasant woman sat in front of her door, reading her hymnbook, the wind turned the pages and said to the book, "Who can be more pious than you?" "Elise!" said the hymnbook: and what the roses and the hymnbook said was the simple truth.

When she was fifteen years old Elise was to go home. But when the Queen saw how beautiful she was, she was filled with hatred towards her. She would gladly have turned her into a wild swan like her brothers, but she did not dare to do so at once, for the King wished to see his daughter.

Early the next morning the Queen went into the great bathroom, which was built of white marble and decked with soft cushions and beautiful rugs. She took three toads, kissed them, and said to the first, "Sit upon Elise's head when she comes into the bath, so

179

that she may become as stupid as you! Sit upon her forehead," she said to the second, "so that she may become as ugly as you, and that her father may not know her. Rest upon her heart," she whispered to the third, "so that she may now have an evil mind and suffer from it."

Then the Queen put the toads into the clear water, which at once turned a green color. Calling Elise, she bade her undress and go into the water. As Elise plunged in, the first toad sat upon her hair, the second on her forehead, and the third on her heart, but she did not seem to notice it. When she rose, three red poppies were seen floating on the water. If the creatures had not been poisonous, and had not been kissed by the witch, they would have been changed into red roses; yet they became flowers because they had rested on Elise's head and heart. She was too good and too innocent for witch-craft to have power over her.

When the wicked Queen saw that, she rubbed Elise with walnut juice so that she became dark brown, smeared a harmful ointment on her face and let her beautiful hair hang in a tangle. No one would have recognized her.

When her father saw her, he was shocked, and declared this was not his daughter. No one recognized her but the dog and the swallows, but they were poor animals who could say nothing.

Then poor Elise wept and thought of her eleven brothers who had disappeared. Sadly she stole out of the castle. She wandered all day over field and moor as far as the great wood. She did not know where to go; but felt very sorrowful, and longed for her brothers; they had probably been, like herself, driven out into the wide world, and she must find them. She had been only a short time in the wood when night fell. She had lost the path, so she lay down upon the soft moss, said her evening prayer and rested her head against the stump of a tree.

The whole night she dreamed of her brothers. They were children again playing together, writing with their diamond pencils upon their golden slates. Only they were not writing lines and letters, as they used to do, but writing of all they had seen and experienced.

When Elise awoke, the sun was already high. She could not see it, for the lofty trees spread their branches above her, but the rays played above like a gauzy veil. She heard the splashing of water from a number of springs all flowing into a lake with the most delightful sandy bottom. It was surrounded by thick bushes, but in one place the deer had trampled a large opening and here Elise could get to the water. It was so clear that every leaf was clearly mirrored on the smooth water.

When Elise saw her own face, she was frightened; it was so brown and ugly; but when she wetted her little hand and rubbed her eyes and forehead, the white skin appeared again. Then she undressed and went down into the fresh water, and a more beautiful King's daughter could not have been found in all the world.

When she had dressed herself again and plaited her long hair, she went to the bubbling spring and drank from the hollow of her hand. Then she wandered deeper into the wood, not knowing where she went. She thought of her brothers, and she knew that Heaven would not forsake her. God had made the wild apples grow to feed the hungry, and He showed her a tree with the boughs bending under the weight of its fruit. Here she took her midday meal and, having propped up the heavy boughs, went into the darkest part of the forest. It was so quiet there that she could hear her own footsteps. Here was such a solitude as she had never before known.

The night came on very dark; not a single glowworm now gleamed in the grass. Sorrowfully Elise lay down to sleep. Then it seemed to her as if the branches above her parted, and the sweet eyes of angels looked down upon her. When morning came she did not know if she had dreamed it, or if it had really been true.

She walked a few steps forward. Then she met an old woman with a basket full of berries. The woman gave her a few of them, and Elise asked her if she had not seen eleven Princes riding through the wood.

"No," replied the old woman, "but yesterday I saw eleven swans, with golden crowns on their heads, swimming down the stream close by."

She led Elise a little further on, to where a little river wound its way. The trees on either side stretched their long leafy branches toward each other. Elise said good-by to the old woman, and followed the river to the place where it flowed out to the open ocean.

The whole glorious sea lay before the young Princess' eyes, but not a sail appeared, not a single boat was to be seen. How was she to go on? She looked at the countless little pebbles on the shore which the water had worn quite smooth. Glass, iron, stones, all that had been washed up had been rounded by the water which was even softer than Elise's delicate hands.

"It rolls on unweariedly, and thus what is hard becomes smooth. I will be just as unwearied! Thanks for your lesson, you clear rolling waves! My heart tells me that one day you will lead me to my dear brothers."

On the sea-grass lay eleven white swan's feathers, which she collected. Drops of water were on them—whether they were dewdrops or tears she could not tell. It was very lonely there, but she did not mind it, for the sea was ever changing.

When the sun was just about to set, Elise saw eleven wild swans, with golden crowns on their heads, flying toward the land; they swept along, one behind the other, so that they looked like a long white band. She climbed down the slope and hid herself behind a bush. The swans alighted near her and flapped their great white wings.

As soon as the sun had disappeared beneath the water, the swans' feathers fell off, and there stood eleven handsome Princes, Elise's brothers. She uttered a loud cry, for although they were greatly altered, she knew them. She sprang into their arms, and called them by their names. The Princes were overjoyed when they saw their little sister again; they knew her, too, though she was now tall and beautiful. They laughed and wept, and soon understood how cruel their stepmother had been to them all.

"We brothers," said the eldest, "fly about as wild swans as long

as the sun is in the sky, but when it has set we return to our human form. Therefore at sunset we must take care to have ground under our feet, for if we were then flying up among the clouds, we would sink into the sea as men. We do not live here. A land just as fair as this lies beyond this sea. But it is far and we must cross the mighty ocean to reach it, and on the way there is no island where we could pass the night. But one single little rock rises from the waves; it is just large enough for us to rest upon it close to one another. If the sea is rough, the foam spurts over us, yet we thank God for the rock. There we pass the night in our human form; were it not for this rock, we could never visit our beloved native land, for the journey requires two of the longest days in the year. Only once each year can we visit our home, and then we dare stay only eleven days. When we fly over the great wood we can see the Palace in which we were born and in which our father lives, and the high church tower where our mother lies buried. Here is our own land, to which we feel ourselves drawn—and here we have found you, our dear little sister. Two more days we may stay here; then we must fly over the sea to a land that is beautiful but is not our native land. How can we bear you away? We have neither ship nor boat."

"How can I release you?" asked the sister.

They went on talking far into the night, sleeping only for a few hours. Elise was awakened by the sound of swans' wings above her. Her brothers were again transformed and flew in wide circles, and, at last, far away. But one of them, the youngest, stayed behind, and the swan laid his head in her lap, and she stroked his wings. They remained together the whole day. Towards evening the others came back, and when the sun had gone down they stood there in their human form.

"Tomorrow we fly far away," they told Elise, "and cannot come back for a whole year. But we cannot leave you like this! Have you the courage to come with us? Should not all our wings be strong enough to carry you over the sea?"

"Yes, take me with you!" cried Elise.

That whole night they wove a net of willow bark and tough reeds, and it was great and strong. Elise lay down on this net, and when the sun rose and her brothers were changed into wild swans, they seized the net with their beaks, and flew with their beloved sister who was still asleep high up toward the clouds. The sunbeams fell upon her face, and one of the swans flew over her head to shade her with his broad wings.

They were far from land when Elise awoke. She thought she was still dreaming, for it seemed so strange to be carried through the air, high over the sea. By her side lay a branch with beautiful ripe berries, and a bundle of sweet-tasting roots. The youngest brother had gathered them and placed them there for her. She smiled at him thankfully, for she recognized him; it was he who flew over her and shaded her with his wings.

The whole day they flew on through the air, but their flight was slower than usual, for they had their sister to carry. Bad weather came on. As evening drew near, Elise looked anxiously at the setting sun

184

for the lonely rock in the ocean could not be seen. It seemed to her that the swans beat the air more strongly with their wings. Alas! it was her fault that they could not fly fast enough; at sunset they must become men and fall into the sea and drown. She prayed from the depths of her heart. Dark clouds rolled near; and the lightning burst forth, flash after flash.

Now the sun touched the edge of the sea. Elise's heart trembled. Then suddenly the swans darted downward so swiftly that she thought they were falling. The sun was half hidden below the water. And now for the first time Elise saw the little rock beneath her. It looked no larger than a seal thrusting its head out of the water. The sun sank very fast; at last it seemed only like a star and then Elise's foot touched the rock. The sun went out like the last spark in a burned paper. Her brothers were standing around her, arm in arm—but there was only just room enough for them and her. The sea beat against the rock and over her like small rain, the sky glowing with continual fire while the thunder rolled. Sister and brothers held one another by the hand and sang a psalm, which gave them comfort and courage.

At dawn the air was pure and calm. As soon as the sun rose, the

swans flew away from the island with Elise. When the sun rose higher, Elise saw before her, half floating in the air, a mountainous country with shining masses of ice on the water. In the midst of it rose a castle with row above row of columns. Palm trees swayed below, and there were flowers as large as millwheels. Elise asked if this was the land to which they were bound, but the swans shook their heads, for what she beheld was the gorgeous ever-changing palace of Fata Morgana into which they might bring no human being. As Elise gazed at it, mountain, woods, and castle suddenly crumbled, and in their place stood twenty proud churches, all nearly alike, with high towers and pointed windows. She fancied she heard the sound of organs, but it was the sea she heard. When she was quite near the churches they seemed to change into a fleet of ships sailing beneath her, but when she looked down it was only the sea mist over the ocean. A continual change kept passing before her eyes, till at last she made out the real land to which they were bound. There arose the most glorious blue mountains with cedar forests, cities, and palaces. Long before the sun went down, Elise was sitting on a rock in front of a great cave overgrown with green trailing plants that looked like embroidered carpets.

"Now we shall see what you will dream of here tonight," said the youngest brother, and he showed her where she was to sleep.

"I hope that I may dream of a way to set you free," she replied. This thought possessed her, and she prayed ardently for help; even in her sleep she continued to pray. Then it seemed to her as if she were flying high in the air to the cloudy palace of Fata Morgana; and a fairy came out to meet her, beautiful and radiant. And yet the fairy looked quite like the old woman who had given her the berries in the wood and had told her of the swans with golden crowns on their heads.

"Your brothers can be set free," she said, "but have you courage and perseverance? Water is softer than your delicate hands, and yet it changes the shape of stones, but it does not feel the pain your fingers will feel; it has no heart, and cannot suffer the agony and torment you will have to endure. Do you see the stinging nettle I hold in my hand? This kind grows plentifully around the cave in which you sleep. Those only and those that grow on the graves in the churchyard must be used—remember that! Those you must pluck, though they will burn your hands into blisters. Break these nettles with your feet, and you will have flax. Of this you must plait and weave eleven shirts of mail with long sleeves; throw these over the eleven swans, and the charm will be broken. But listen well: from the moment you begin this work until it is finished, even though it should take years, you must not speak! The first word you utter will pierce your brothers' hearts like a deadly dagger. Their lives hang on your tongue. Remember!"

She touched Elise's hand with the nettles; it was like a burning fire, and Elise woke with the smart. It was broad daylight; and close by the spot where she had slept lay a nettle like the one she had seen in her dream. She fell on her knees and prayed gratefully, and went out from the cave to begin her work.

With her delicate hands she groped among the ugly nettles. They stung like fire, burning great blisters on her arms and hands; but she thought she could bear it gladly if she could only free her dear brothers. Then she crushed every nettle with her bare feet and plaited the green flax.

When the sun had set, her brothers came, and they were frightened when they found her dumb. They thought it was some new sorcery of their wicked stepmother's; but when they saw her hands they understood what she was doing for their sake. The youngest brother wept, and where his tears dropped Elise felt no pain, and the burning blisters vanished.

She worked the whole night, for she could not sleep until she had freed her dear brothers. All the following day, while the swans were away, she sat in solitude, but never had time flown so quickly. One shirt was already finished and now she began the second.

Then a hunting horn sounded in the hills and she was struck with fear. As the noise came nearer, and she heard the barking dogs, she fled into the cave. There she bound into a bundle the nettles she had gathered, and sat upon the bundle.

A big hound came bounding out of the ravine, and then another, and another. They barked loudly, ran back, and then came on again. In a few minutes all the huntsmen stood outside the cave. The handsomest of them was the King of the country. He came forward to Elise, for he had never seen a more beautiful maiden.

"How did you come here, you delightful child?" he asked.

Elise shook her head, for she might not speak—it would cost her brothers their deliverance and their lives. She hid her hands under her apron so that the King might not see what she was suffering.

"Come with me," he said. "You cannot stay here. If you are as good as you are beautiful, I will dress you in velvets and silks and place the golden crown on your head, and you shall dwell in my richest castle and rule."

Then he lifted her onto his horse. Elise wept and wrung her hands, but the King said, "I only wish your happiness; one day you will thank me for this." And placing her behind him on his horse, he galloped away among the mountains, while the huntsmen followed after them.

At sunset the fair regal city, with its churches and cupolas, lay before them. The King led Elise into the castle where great fountains played in the lofty marble halls. The walls and ceilings were covered with glorious pictures. But the poor young Princess had no eyes for all this. She only wept and grieved. Passively she let the women dress her in royal robes, and weave pearls in her hair, and draw soft gloves over her blistered fingers.

When she was fully arrayed, she was so dazzlingly beautiful that the court bowed deeper than before. The King chose her for his bride. But now the King's advisor shook his head and whispered that the beautiful maid was certainly a witch, who blinded the eyes and led astray the King's heart.

The King gave no heed to this. He ordered that music should

sound, and the costliest dishes be served, and that the most beautiful maidens should dance before him and his betrothed. Elise was led through fragrant gardens into gorgeous halls; but never a smile came to her lips or shone in her eyes. There she stood, a picture of grief. Then the King opened the door to a little chamber close by, where she was to sleep. It was decked with green tapestry, to resemble the cave in which the King had found her. On the floor lay the bundle of flax she had prepared from the nettles, and from the ceiling hung the shirt of mail she had completed. One of the huntsmen had brought these things with him as curiosities.

"Here you may dream yourself back in your former home," said the King. "Here is the work you were doing there. Now, in the midst of all your splendor, it will amuse you to think of that time."

When Elise saw these things that were so dear to her heart, a smile played around her mouth, and the blood came back into her cheeks. She thought of her brothers' deliverance, and kissed the King's hand. He pressed her to his heart, and ordered all the church bells to announce the marriage feast. The beautiful dumb girl out of the wood was to be Queen of the country!

Then the King's advisor again whispered evil words in the King's ear, but again they did not sink into the King's heart. The marriage would take place. The King's advisor himself was obliged to place the crown on Elise's head, and with wicked spite he pressed the narrow circlet so tightly upon her brow that it hurt her. But a heavier ring lay around her heart; sorrow for her brothers. She remained dumb, for a single word would have cost her brothers their lives. But her eyes glowed with love for the kind, handsome King who did everything to please her. She loved him with her whole heart, more and more every day. Oh, if she could only confide in him of her grief! But she must remain dumb and finish her work in silence. Therefore at night she stole away from his side and went quietly to the little chamber that was decorated like the cave, and wove one shirt of mail after another. But when she began the seventh she had no flax left to finish it.

She knew that the nettles she could use were growing in the churchyard, but she must pluck them herself, and how was she to go out there?

"Oh, what is the pain in my fingers compared with the torment my heart endures!" she thought. "I must venture it, and help will not be denied me!" With a trembling heart, as though she were doing something evil, she crept into the garden one moonlight night and through the lanes and the deserted streets to the churchyard. There she saw a circle af lamias sitting on one of the broadest tombstones. These hideous wretches took off their rags as if they were going to bathe; then with their skinny fingers they clawed open the fresh graves. Elise had to pass close by them, and they fastened their evil eyes upon her, but she prayed silently and gathered the burning nettles, and carried them back to the castle.

Only one person had seen her and that was the King's advisor. He was awake while the others slept. Now he felt sure that all was not as it should be with the Queen. She was a witch and she had bewitched the King and the whole people.

In secret, he told the King what he had seen and what he feared, and as he spoke these hard words, the pictures of saints in the cathedral shook their heads, as though they said: "It is not true, Elise is innocent." But the King's advisor chose to interpret this differently; he said they were bearing witness against her, and shaking their heads at her sinfulness. Then two heavy tears rolled down the King's cheeks; he went home with doubt in his heart. At night he pretended to be asleep, but no peace came to him for he noticed that Elise got up every night. Each time he followed her silently and saw how she disappeared from her chamber.

Now she had almost finished her work; only one shirt of mail remained to be completed, but she had no flax left and not a single nettle. Once more, for the last time, she must go to the churchyard to pluck a few handfuls of nettles. She thought with terror of the horrible lamias, but her will was as firm as her trust in Providence.

Elise went, but the King and his advisor followed her. They saw her vanish through the gate into the churchyard, and when they drew near, the lamias were sitting on the tombstone as Elise had seen them. The King turned away, for he imagined she was amongst them—she whose head had rested against his breast that very evening.

"The people must judge her," he said. And the people condemned her to suffer death by fire.

Out of the regal halls she was led into a dark damp cell, where the wind whistled through the barred window. Instead of silk and velvet she was given the bundle of nettles she had gathered. She was to lay her head upon this, and the hard burning coats of mail were to be her coverlet. But she was not dismayed; indeed, she could not have been given anything that would have pleased her more. She started her work again, and prayed. Outside, the boys on the street were singing jeering songs about her, and not a soul comforted her with a kind word.

But toward evening there came the whirring of a swan's wings close to the grating; it was the youngest of her brothers. Elise sobbed aloud for joy, though she knew that the coming night might be the last she had to live; however, her work was almost done, and her brothers were here.

Now the King's advisor came to stay with her in her last hour, for he had promised the King to do so. But Elise shook her head, and with looks and gestures begged him to leave her. For in this night she must finish her work, or all would have been in vain—all her suffering, and all her tears. The King's advisor withdrew, uttering evil words against her; but poor Elise knew she was innocent, and went on with her work.

It was still an hour before sunrise when the eleven brothers stood at the castle gate and demanded to be brought before the King. This could not be done, they were told, for the King was asleep and might not be disturbed. They begged and they threatened and the sentries turned out, and even the King himself came out and asked what the disturbance meant. At that moment the sun rose and the brothers were no more to be seen, but eleven wild swans were seen flying away over the castle.

All the people came streaming out at the town gate to see the

192

witch burned. An old horse drew the cart on which Elise sat. She had been clothed in a garment of coarse sackcloth; her lovely hair hung loose about her beautiful head; her cheeks were pale as death, and her lips moved silently while her fingers busied themselves with the green flax. Even on the way to her death she did not interrupt the work she had begun. The ten shirts of mail lay at her feet and she was working on the eleventh.

The mob jeered, "Look at the witch, how she mutters! She has no hymn-book in her hand, no—it's her ugly sorcery, that's what she's holding. Tear it in a thousand pieces!"

They all pressed upon her to tear up the shirts of mail. Suddenly eleven white swans swept down, sat round about her on the cart, and beat with their great wings. The mob fell back before them, terrified.

"That is a sign from heaven! She is innocent!" many whispered. But they did not dare to say it aloud.

Now the executioner seized Elise by the hand, but she hastily threw the eleven shirts over the swans, and in a twinkling eleven handsome Princes stood there. But the youngest had a swan's wing instead of an arm, for Elise had not quite finished the second sleeve of his shirt.

"Now I may speak!" she said. "I am innocent."

And the people who saw what had happened bowed before her as before a saint. But she sank as if lifeless into the arms of her brothers. The suspense, the anguish, and the pain had exhausted her.

"Yes, she is innocent," said the eldest brother, and he told them all that had happened. While he spoke, a fragrance arose of millions of roses, for every fagot at the stake had taken root and put forth branches, and a great fragrant hedge appeared covered with red roses. At the top was a single white flower, shining and gleaming like a star. The King picked this flower and laid it on Elise's bosom, and she arose with peace and happiness in her heart.

And all the church bells rang out of their own accord, and birds came in great flocks. And back to the castle went a magnificent procession.

Rip Van Winkle

ILLUSTRATED BY DARLEY

ANYONE WHO HAS SAILED up the Hudson River must remember the Kaatskill Mountains. They can be seen away to the west of the river, rising up to a noble height, their blue and purple outlines sharp against the clear evening sky. But sometimes, even on a cloudless day, gray mists swirl about their peaks, and many tales are told about strange happenings in these mysterious mountains.

In a quiet little village nestling at the foot of these mountains there lived, many years ago, a simple, good-natured fellow named Rip Van Winkle. He was a kind and helpful neighbor, and an obedient, henpecked husband.

Rip was a great favorite with everyone in the village, always ready to lend a helping hand or go on errands for the housewives. The children of the village especially would shout with joy whenever they saw him. He helped them in their sports, made playthings for the younger ones, taught them to fly kites and shoot marbles, and told them endless stories of witches and Indians, and of ghosts that were said to haunt the deep, wild places in the surrounding mountains. Whenever he went ambling about the village he was surrounded by a troop of children, and not a dog would bark at him in the whole neighborhood.

Rip had, however, one great fault: he was averse to doing any kind of work, either on his farm, or around his house. As a result, his farm and farmhouse were sadly neglected, and his children ran about ragged and wild, as if they belonged to nobody. His son, Rip, gave promise of inheriting the habits, along with the old clothes, of his father.

Rip Van Winkle, however, was one of those happy people who take the world easy, and he would have been perfectly content, but for his scolding wife. Dame Van Winkle kept continually dinning in his ears the ruin he was bringing on his family by his idleness and carelessness. Morning, noon and night, her tongue was incessantly going. His only answer was to shrug his shoulders, cast up his eyes, and finally to pick up his hunting gun and take to the outside of the house.

His sole domestic comfort was his dog, Wolf, who was as much henpecked as his master, for Dame Van Winkle considered them companions in idleness. Wolf was courageous enough when he scoured the woods, but the moment he entered the house his tail drooped to the ground or curled between his legs, and he sneaked about keeping a cautious eye on Dame Van Winkle. At the least motion of her broomstick he would fly to the door.

When driven from home, Rip used to console himself by joining up with other idlers of the village. They would gather on a bench in front of a small inn whose sign showed a portrait of His Majesty George the Third. Here they would sit in the shade through a long lazy summer's day, talking listlessly over the village gossip, or just telling sleeping stories about nothing.

But even here Rip was not safe from his wife's scolding tongue. She would suddenly break in upon the quiet group:

"I thought I'd find you here!"

Then she would turn on his companions:

"And the rest of you are no better than he is!"

But if she hoped she could get Rip to mend his ways, and come home to the chores that needed to be done on his farm, she was mistaken. Instead, in despair, he would pick up his gun, call his faithful dog Wolf to him, and stroll away into the woods.

On one fine autumn day Rip had gone for a long ramble of this kind. Without noticing where his feet were leading him, he found himself in a wild spot in one of the highest parts of the Kaatskill Mountains. He was enjoying his favorite sport of squirrel shooting, and all afternoon the sound of his gun had echoed through the still woods. At last, late in the afternoon, panting and tired, he threw himself on a green knoll that jutted out over a precipice. From an

opening between the trees he could look out over all the lower country for miles around. Beyond the rich woodland, he could see the lordly Hudson River far, far below him, moving on its majestic course. On the other side he looked down into a deep mountain glen, wild, lonely and rugged.

For some time Rip lay enjoying this scene. Evening was gradually coming on. Now the mountains began to throw their long blue shadows across the valleys, and he saw that it would be dark before he could reach the village. He heaved a heavy sigh when he thought of the scolding he would be sure to get from Dame Van Winkle.

As he was getting ready to go down he thought he heard a voice calling from a distance:

"Rip Van Winkle! Rip Van Winkle!"

He looked around, but all he saw was a crow winging its solitary flight across the mountain. He decided he must have imagined the call. But when he turned to continue down the mountain, he heard the same cry ring through the still evening air:

"Rip Van Winkle! Rip Van Winkle!"

Now Wolf bristled up his back, and with a low growl skulked to his master's side, looking fearfully down into the glen. At the same time a low roll of thunder seemed to come up from the ravine, though there was no hint of rain in the clear evening sky.

Rip now felt a vague fear stealing over him. He looked anxiously in the direction from which the call had seemed to come. A strange figure was slowly toiling up the rocks, bending under the weight of something he carried on his back. Rip was surprised to see any human being in this lonely place. But he supposed it must be some neighbor in need of his assistance, so he hurried down.

As he came nearer he was still more surprised at the stranger's appearance. He was a short, square-built old fellow with thick bushy hair and a grizzled beard, and he was dressed in old-fashioned Dutch breeches. He was carrying on his shoulder a stout keg that seemed full of a liquid of some kind. He paused in his climb, and made signs for Rip to come and help him with his load.

Rip was still vaguely frightened, and not very trustful of this odd little man. Still, as the fellow seemed to need help, and continued to beckon him, he finally went down into the glen, and together they clambered up a narrow gully, carrying the keg between them. As they climbed, Rip was dismayed to hear, every now and then, long rolling peals like distant thunder that seemed to come out of a deep ravine. They toiled upward for a while in complete silence, until they came to a hollow that looked like a small amphitheatre, surrounded by steep, sheer sides of rock.

Here Rip was astonished to see a whole assemblage of odd-looking men. They were playing at nine-pins on a level spot in the center of the hollow. Like the stranger whom Rip had helped up the gully, they were dressed in outlandish fashion; some wore short doublets, others jerkins, with long knives in their belts, and most of them had enormous breeches like those worn by the guide. They all had beards of various shapes and colors. One stout gentleman with a weather-beaten face seemed to be the commander.

What seemed to Rip particularly strange was that, though they seemed to be amusing themselves with a game, they all had the gravest faces, and all kept a most mysterious silence. He thought this was the saddest-looking pleasure party he had ever seen. Nothing interrupted the stillness but the noise of the balls, which, whenever they were rolled, echoed along the mountains like rumbling peals of thunder.

As Rip and his companion approached, the men suddenly stopped their play and stared at him. His companion now emptied the contents of the keg into large flagons, and made signs for Rip to wait upon the company. He obeyed with fear and trembling. They drank the liquid in profound silence, and then went back to their game.

After a while Rip began to feel easier. No longer fearful, he even ventured, when no one was looking, to taste the liquid. He was delighted to find that it had an excellent flavor. A naturally thirsty soul, he was soon tempted to sample another draught. One taste provoked another, and he repeated his visits to the flagon so often that at last he began to feel both giddy and drowsy. His eyes swam, his head began to nod, and he gradually sank to the ground and fell into a deep sleep.

When he awoke, he found himself on the same green knoll where he had been when he first saw the old man of the glen. He rubbed his eyes—it was a bright sunny morning.

"Surely," he thought, "I have not slept here all night!"

He began to recall all the strange things that had taken place before he fell asleep: the man with the keg—the mountain ravine and the wild hollow among the rocks—the woebegone party playing at nine-pins—the flagon ——

"Oh! that flagon! that wicked flagon!" thought Rip. "What excuse shall I make to Dame Van Winkle?"

He looked around for his gun. But in place of the clean well-oiled fowling-piece, he found an old firelock lying near him, the barrel incrusted with rust and the stock worm-eaten. Now he suspected that those silent nine-pin players had played a trick on him; they had drugged him with their mysterious liquid and robbed him of his gun. Wolf, too, had disappeared.

He called aloud:

"Here Wolf—Wolf!"

He tried to whistle up the dog, but his lips were too dry and cracked to pucker. After a few minutes, he reflected that the dog might have strayed away after a squirrel or a partridge.

He decided to go back to the place where he had watched the nine-pin players the evening before. If he could find any of the party, he would demand his dog and his gun. As he rose to walk, however, he found himself stiff in the joints. He could straighten up only with difficulty.

"These mountain beds do not agree with me," thought Rip. "And what will Dame Van Winkle say when she sees me like this? I had better go and clean up before I present myself to her."

With some difficulty he got down into the glen. He found the gully up which he and his companion had climbed the evening before, but to his surprise a mountain stream was now foaming down it. At last he reached the place where the ravine had opened through the cliffs, and was astonished to find no trace of such an opening. There was only a wall of rock, over which a torrent of water tumbled into a deep basin. Here, then, poor Rip stopped. Again he called his dog:

"Wolf! Here, Wolf!"

He was answered only by the cawing of a flock of crows flying high in the air above a dead tree. What should he do? The morning was half gone, and Rip felt famished. He was badly in need of his breakfast. He hated to give up his dog and his gun; he dreaded to meet his wife; but neither did he wish to starve in the mountains. So, shouldering the rusty firelock with a heavy heart, he started toward home.

As he drew near the village he met a number of people, but none whom he knew. This surprised him, for he had thought he knew everyone in the country around. He noticed, too, that they were dressed in a fashion different from what he was accustomed to. They all stared at him with equal surprise. Whenever they looked at him they invariably stroked their chins. The constant repetition of this gesture made Rip, involuntarily, do the same. To his astonishment, he found his beard had grown a foot long!

Now he entered the village. A troop of strange children began to follow him, hooting and pointing at his gray beard and rusty gun. The dogs, too—not one of which he recognized—barked at him as he passed. Even the village itself had changed: it seemed larger, and there were many more people. There were rows of houses which he had never seen before, and his familiar haunts had disappeared. Strange names were over the doors—strange faces at the windows—everything was strange.

Rip began to wonder whether both he and the world around him were bewitched. Surely this was his native village which he had left only the day before! There stood the Kaatskill Mountains—there,

in the distance, ran the silvery Hudson River—there was every hill and dale precisely as it had always been. Rip tried to think, but only grew more perplexed.

"That flagon last night," he thought, "has certainly addled my poor head!"

With some difficulty he now made his way to his own house. He approached it timidly, expecting every moment to hear the shrill voice of Dame Van Winkle. There was the house; but to his great dismay he saw that everything had fallen into decay: the roof had fallen in, the windows were shattered, and the doors were off the hinges. A half-starved dog that looked like Wolf was skulking about it. Rip called him by name, but the cur snarled, and slunk away.

"Even my dog," sighed poor Rip, "has forgotten me!"

He entered the house, which Dame Van Winkle had always kept in such neat order. It was empty and apparently abandoned. Suddenly his desolation overcame his fears. He called loudly for his wife and children. The empty rooms echoed his voice, and then all was silence.

He hurried from the house, and sought his old resort—the village inn. But it, too, was gone. A large, rickety wooden building stood in its place, and a painted sign over the door read: "The Union Hotel, Jonathan Doolittle, Proprietor." He recognized on the sign, however, the familiar red-cheeked face of King George; but even this was oddly changed. The red coat was now blue and buff; instead of a sceptre the hand now held a sword; and underneath was painted in large letters: GENERAL WASHINGTON.

There was, as usual, a crowd around the door, but no one that Rip recognized. The very character of the people seemed to have changed. There was a busy bustling tone instead of the customary drowsy tranquility. He looked in vain for his old friend, Nicholas Vedder, with his broad face, double chin, and long pipe. A lean, sour-looking fellow, with his pockets full of handbills, was making a speech to the crowd about the rights of citizens, elections, members of Congress, Liberty, heroes of Seventy-six, and other matters which the bewildered Van Winkle did not understand.